Stephen Moralee

Gone to Flowers...everyone

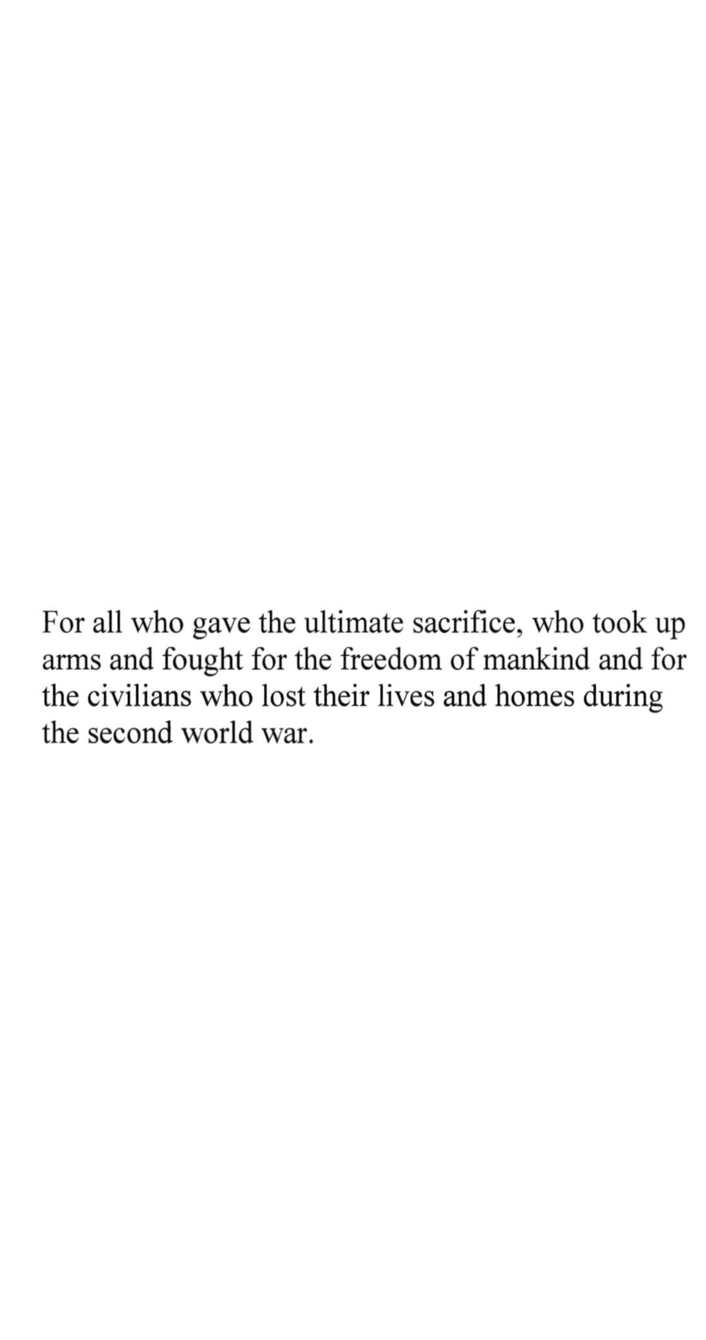

For all who gave the ultimate sacrifice, who took up arms and fought for the freedom of mankind and for the civilians who lost their lives and homes during the second world war.

Stephen Moralee

*Gone to
Flowers...everyone*

Bibliografische Information der Deutschen Nationalbibliothek:
Die Deutsche Nationalbibliothek verzeichnet diese Publikation in der Deutschen Nationalbibliografie; detaillierte bibliografische Daten sind im Internet über http://dnb.dnb.de abrufbar.

Herstellung und Verlag: BoD – Books on Demand, Norderstedt

ISBN: 9 783753 442860

The Peace Child

When the distant thunder of the guns fell silent and
the warm summer winds carried whispers of hope.

When the tired warrior rests on the war scarred earth
and the peace child wakes again.

Time will heal all wounds she says, picking flowers
where her warrior now lays.

But when the summer breeze of hope turns cold and
leaves of hatred fall.

And as the peace child dances one last dance, her
warrior wakes, standing proud and tall.

Weapons ready to silence the threat. Armour shining
in the last peaceful sunset.

And the peace child lays to rest again, and whispers.

„When will you ever learn"
„When will you ever learn"

(Stephen Moralee)

The fallen Imperium

In the final months of World War Two, Japan was bracing itself for one last attack, an anticipated invasion of its country. The once feared military power of the Japanese imperium was almost totally destroyed and most of the Japanese population were suffering from malnutrition and disease caused by the war and the capital city, Tokyo had been reduced to a pile of burning rubble.

The anticipated invasion, would however, never be executed, the option being too dangerous for the allied troops and the expected high casualty count would be unacceptable in the late stages of the war. The actual final attack on Japan in the last days of the Second World War, would however, turn out to be more devastating than anyone could imagine.

The first atomic bomb, known as „Little Boy“ was dropped on Hiroshima on August the 6th 1945. to be followed only a few days later by a second bomb known as „Fat Man“ which was detonated over Nagasaki. The attacks caused an estimated 250,000 civilian deaths, more than a million refugees and Japans eventual surrender.

Many scientists who were involved in the development of the atomic bomb, when realizing how devastating these weapons would be when detonated and the long term consequences of using them in a theatre of war, were against the use of them and **Leo Szilard** one of the key scientists on the Manhattan Project, drafted a petition in the spring of 1945 to try and stop the use of the atomic bombs in Japan.

Unfotunateley the petition failed, paving the way for the destruction of Hiroshima and Nagasaki and the start signal for a nuclear arms race, later to be known as the „Cold War" had been sounded.

The story

„Gone to Flowers...everyone"

was inspired by and is dedicated to the 70 courageous scientists who signed the Szilard petition.

<u>Gone to Flowers...everyone</u>
<u>The Will</u>

It was a late warm August morning in 1992 and Manchester was slowly awakening to the sounds of children making their way to school and car doors being closed as people drove of to go about their daily business. Denise Lawrence was having breakfast after getting ready for work when she heard the clacking sound of the post being delivered through the slit in the front door of her small, red bricked terraced house. She put her coffee down on the kitchen table and went to see what bills she wouldn't be able to pay this time, and let out a sigh of relief when she saw that only a few advertisement brochures, a letter from a friend in London and the morning paper were all that was scattered on the floor in the hallway.

After gathering up the post and making her way back into the kitchen, she noticed a very official looking envelope that had been hidden between a brochure for one of the local supermarkets and the daily paper. She frowned, wondering who the letter was from and turned the envelope around and saw that the sender was a lawyers office in London.

„Hm, what could this be.?" she asked herself as she opened the envelope with a queezy feeling in her stomach. Apart from a few outstanding debts, that weren't all that bad, she couldn't think of why someone should want to set a lawyer on to her and after reading the contents of the letter she was more confused than she was before she had opened it.

It was an invitation from a lawyers office in London, explaining that she had inherited the assets of her deceased parents, Jenny Chandler and Peter Marshall.

„Jenny Chandler and Peter Marshall, who the hell are they?" She asked herself out loud. She had no idea who these people were and her first thoughts were that the whole thing was some kind of joke, or could even be a mistake.

After finishing breakfast she put the letter into her handbag and made her way outside. She closed and locked the front door of her house and made her way to the bus stop at the end of the street. Still wondering about the strange, very official looking envelope and the contents of the letter inside, she decided to get in touch with the lawyer as soon as possible.

She couldn't help smiling as she walked past the chimney smoking, bay windowed terraced houses and the sounds of her neighbourhood, children's voices and people greeting each other in that friendly way made her happy and feel secure. Now and then she brushed her long, dark brown hair out of her face, only for it to be blown back by the warm breeze a few moments later. She eventually put her handbag on the pavement between her feet, took a hairband out one of the back pockets of her jeans and gathered her hair into a pony tail. She heard somebody wolf-whistle and wondered if the whistling was meant for her. She decided that it was and smiled again, promising herself to get a new hairdo with less fringe a soon as she could afford one.

As she arrived at the bus stop, she turned around and looked at the street that she had lived in most of her adult life.

„It isn't perfect, but it is home." She thought to herself as she sat down in one of the plastic seats to wait for the bus.

During her dinner break later that day, she sat in her favourite Cafe and read through the lawyers letter again. It definitely didn't seem like a joke, and if it was , it was done very professionally. But she didn't know who these people were, had never heard of them before and they couldn't have been her parents. Bill and Katy Lawrence were her mum and dad, and have always been as long as she could remember, not this Jenny Chandler, Peter Marshall or anyone else for that matter. She folded the letter back into the envelope and decided to get in touch with the lawyer as soon as she got back home, to let them know that they had made a mistake.

„Brian Thomas, heritage Lawyers." A man answered the phone in a very young sounding London accent. Denise frowned and glanced down at the letter.

„If this was a joke, how would he know that it was her ringing and not someone else?" She thought. „But why would a lawyer answer the phone by himself, usually they had a good looking young assistant to do all the dirty work for them and never really had the time to answer the phone themselves anyway and the „silly Prank" or „joke" idea was beginning to seem more feasible than a mistake or even the fact that the whole thing could even be true. She thought about her old university gang, most of them had a weird sense of houmor and it was her 50 th birthday in a few days, maybe it was a set up for a surprise birthday party?" She shook her head, trying to clear her thoughts.

„Yes, good evening this is Denise Lawrence calling, I received a letter from you this morning and want to clear things up." She said.

„Ah, I'm glad you have got in touch so quickly Mrs Lawrence, we have contacted you on behalf of an American colleague and want to invite you to London to receive the will of your deceased parents, Jenny Chandler and Peter Marshall. Jenny chandler died a while ago and Peter Marshall went missing in 1945 near the coast of Japan and was presumed dead shortly after the end of the second world war." Brian explained.

Denise asked him if he was sure, as she had never heard of these people and they definitely couldn't have been her parents.

There was a pregnant pause and she heard the sound of the shuffling of paper.

„This is no Lawyer" She thought to herself and felt sorry for this poor bloke who was probably the son of one of her student gang and had been told to play out this prank.

„You are Mrs, Lawrence, daughter of Bill and Katy Lawrence, who moved from San Francisco to re settle in Manchester in 1964?" Brian asked.

„Yes that's me, Bill and Katy are my.....were my mum and dad, mum died ten years ago and dad last year... and if this is some kind of silly prank I am not amused because it is definitely not funny at all." The thoughts of her mum and dad had made her feel quite angry and she wasn't really sure if one of her Friends would do this kind of thing to her. There was another pregnant pause, she heard the shuffling of paper again and Brian whispering to someone. After a few moments that felt to her like 10 minutes until he came back on to the phone.

„Mrs Lawrence, I can assure you that this is no joke and i think you should make your way to London as soon as possible, we have very important information for you." Brian said, now sounding very official and much more like a Lawyer.

„OK, I have a day off in three days because it's my birthday, I can be in London by late morning." Denise said.

Three days later she was sitting in a very comfortable leather chair in Brian Thomas's office. Sitting opposite was a very scruffy looking young Lawyer and his not all that good looking assistant who was called Chantalle.

Brian Thomas lay two Envelopes on the huge Oak Table, cleared his voice and nodded to Denise as he opened the first Envelope.

„In the case of my death, I leave all my assets, Land and contents of my bank accounts in Los Angeles and Chicago to Mrs Jenny Chandler."

Signed, Peter Marshall on 23.11.1941

Brian then opened the second envelope, nodded again and read the second will.

„In the case of my death, I leave the contents of Peter Marshall's will, from 23.12.1941 to our daughter Denise Lawrence, who should not be informed of this will as long as her adoptive parents are still alive."

Signed, Jenny Chandler on 14.01.1946

„As the four are now deceased, Peter Marshall's assets now belong to you, Mrs Lawrence." Brian Thomas said, nodding again to Denise, who was now looking at him as if she needed to ask an important question.

„We will cover any inquiries when i am finished"
Brian said before reading out a third document.

*„Denise Lawrence, Daughter of the deceased Jenny
Chandler and missing, presumed dead Peter
Marshall is to receive the following.*

Land in California worth 6,5 million Dollars.

*Bank account contents in Los Angeles and Chicago
worth 4,2 Million Dollars*

*Assets and company shares in the following
companies.*

*Marshall real estate, Chandler Real estate and the
LA times newspaper, worth together 3 Million
dollars. "*

Brian's assistant Chantalle, nodded to Denise.

„Mrs Lawrence I am not sure if you have realized,
but your life will never be the same again after
today......"

„Almost 14 Million Dollars!"' Denise butted in.
„Are you sure there is no mistake?" She asked.

„Yes we check these things very carefully Mrs
Lawrence." The girl replied. „We advise you think
carefully what you want to do with the assets and we
have been assigned to assist you on any legal
matters, of course you can deny our help if it is not
required, the Bank account contents in Los Angeles
and Chicago can be moved to your UK account

within a few days." Chantalle added and nodded to Denise and then to Brian who nodded back.
Denise wondered if this nodding thing was some kind of ritual that only Lawyers do in meetings or if they both had the same illness that forced them to nod each time they open their mouths.

„Yes I think that would be a good idea and of course I am quite happy for you to cover any legal matters for me." Denise said and Smiled at Brian and Chantalle who both nodded in agreement and Denise was trying hard now, not to burst out laughing at the pair of them.

Thousands of chimneys

For most of the train journey back to Manchester Denise didn't think once about the wealth she had inherited or that her life had changed forever. It was the thought that she was adopted and Katy and Bill weren't her real parents that had locked itself in the back room of her mind and wasn't letting anything else in. When she eventually arrived home she made herself a coffee and began write a to do list.

Quit Job, get a Car, get a new hairdo....

She had to laugh at the fact that getting a hairdo was one of the most important things on her agenda and paused for a while to sit back and look out of the kitchen window at the rows of terraced houses, the roofs now changing colour in the sunset.

She had actually painted a picture of this very scene some years ago and had called it „Thousands of chimneys" She thought about her first art exhibition as a student in London where critics had said that her work was very similar to that of the Manchester artist L.S. Lowry. She smiled and began to hum the tune of „Match stalk men and match stalk cats and dogs" a well known folk song in the seventies about Lowry and his art work. She looked out of the window again at the town she had fallen in love with as a young woman and began to sing.

„He painted Salfords smokey tops, on cardboard boxes from the shops, and parts of Ancoats where i used to play"

The smell of coffee and children playing outside in the street and the thoughts of her adoptive parents who had always been very kind and loving to her, bought her back into the present.

„They had never been rich and weren't interested in material things, but had made her childhood worth more money than this Jenny Chandler could ever pass on to her." She thought, as a tear ran down her face and dropped onto the to do list. She thought about her childhood in California and how Bill and Katy had always been there for her no matter what and was disgusted that her real mother, Jenny Chandler had given her up for adoption almost fifty years ago and that her real Father, this Peter Marshall probably didn't care less about her, or didn't even know she existed.

"It would be more challenging to come to terms with that than getting used to being rich all of a sudden." She thought as she read through the will again.

„Written on 23.12.1941." She thought.

„Hmm, I was born end of August 1942, nine months later." Denise frowned.

„My real father coldnt have been much older than thirty at the time, so why would he think that he

might die, was it possible that he knew he was going
to be doing something dangerous or...go to war?"
She thought out loud, her voice echoing through the
kitchen causing a cold shiver to go down her spine.
„Of course, December 1941 was the attack on Pearl
Harbour, Shortly after that the Americans joined the
Allies in the second world war.... missing presumed
dead." She said quietly to herself, scratching her
head and sitting back into the kitchen stool.

Either he knew he was going to die, or at least there
was a danger of that happening, or.... he knew he
was going to be presumed dead. Had her father used
the situation to get away from the life he was having,
to get away from the responsibilities of caring for a
small child and make a new start somewhere totally
different, or was he on the run?" the more she
thought about it the more unanswered questions flew
into her mind.

She thought about what Brian Thomas had said as he
drove her back to Kings Cross Station.

„Your real Father, Peter Marshal, was a scientist and
involved in a military project in the 1940s, he was
apparently piloting a plane on a secret mission a few
days before the end of the war when he went
missing and shortly after the war he was presumed
dead". Brian parked his car on one of the taxi stands
at the main entrance of Kings cross and handed her a
further brown envelope.

„All the information our colleagues in America
could gather about your father is in this document, it

now belongs to you." He said.

She thought about Jenny Chandler and the fact that she had passed on the will of her father, Peter Marshall, knowing full well how much money it was worth. Which made her think twice about what kind of person she was,or could have been.

„OK, so she wasn't greedy, or she was rich anyway and didn't need the money." She thought and tried to weigh up the whole situation and how life could have been back in the days of the second world war. The fact that Jenny had given her up for adoption still disgusted her, but she was happy that Katy had given her everything she could have wanted, her adoptive father too.

„But who was her real Father, what kind of person was Peter Marshall and what was he doing off the coast of Japan in the last days of the war... Presumed dead?... is it possible that he survived the war, maybe he is still alive and if he is...where is he?" The more she thought about him, the more unanswered questions jumped into her mind, queueing up to be answered.

She decided that finding out as much as she could about Peter Marshall was the most important thing to do and threw the tear stained list into the bin.

The following morning she got in touch with her best friend, Jane, to tell her all about what had happened in London and about her Mysterious father.

She also told her boss at work about the will and although he was sad to see her go, agreed that she now had more important things to do than to get up every morning and go to work. She also decided to keep her small house, it was warm, cosy and reminded her of Bill and Katy and her childhood.

The smell of freshly baked apple pie, the coal fires and smoking chimneys, washing hanging out in the small back yards and the BBC Saturday morning show echoing around the neighbourhood from radios that were placed on the sills of open kitchen windows, were the things that had made her happy as a young woman here in Manchester and right now she had no interest in changing that scenario.

<u>Jane</u>

A few days later Denise invited her friend Jane over for tea and to help her make a plan to try and find out all she could about her mysterious father.

„I have found out that he studied physics at Oxford University in the 1920s, that he was in the Oxford rowing team and was the son of a rich Architect from Chicago, who he worked for after finishing his studies in England. He then moved to LA to write a scientific column in the LA Times News Paper in 1935, he was quite famous in the States." Denise explained to Jane, while she was taking her jacket off and making her way into the kitchen.

„I also contacted the US Military who informed me that he left LA in 1941 to work on some kind of military project and the only other information they could give me was that he was pronounced missing off the Japanese coast and shortly after the war was over, was assumed to have perished while carrying out a secret mission. The lawyer in London had most of that information too, but between 1941 and 1945, nobody seems to know where he was or what exactly he was up to and I think if I could find that out, maybe I would get a step further in finding out what happened to him. The mission was so secret that it wasn't even documented so that cannot even be confirmed." she explained to Jane as they cooked the dinner together.

„Hmm Presumed dead...so they didn't find his body and cant really confirm that he died on that mission,?" Jane asked.

„Yes that's the information I have from the Lawyer and the Military in the states." Denise answered.

„I think you might get more accurate information if you went to LA and checked out where he worked and lived, somebody who knew him well back then might be able to help out more. I'm not sure if the military is too keen on giving out information on secret missions that they carried out." Jane said as they set the table.

„Where did he go after leaving LA, maybe the name of the project he was involved in, things like that." she added as she took a sip of fruit juice and tucked into the bangers and mash tea.

„Hmm give me the brown sauce, this is lovely." Jane then said, rolling her eyes and smiling at Denise.

„Jane, help me find my father, I don't know anybody who I can trust as much as you and I need a helping hand on this one." Denise said.

Jane had been made redundant a few months earlier and was back living with her parents, the idea of having an excuse for getting out and about now and then was definitely appealing to her.

„Living with mum and dad is like hell for me, and I need something to do, just to get away now and then." Jane said.

„You can live here in my house, I will pay you well, money is no problem." Denise said smiling.

Denise would have given her best friend enough money so that she wouldn't have had to have work another day in her life anyway.

They had met the day Denise moved to England with her parents all those years ago, were best friends within five minutes and have been ever since. Jane had been there for Denise when her marriage broke up and when Jane's Husband died in a car accident, Denise had dropped everything, took time off work and did everything she could to help her and she knew Jane would do the same for her too.

 „Oh love, you have just saved my life." Jane said.

„Well its not quite all that dramatic, and I think we are going to have enough to do trying to find out what happened to my Father." Denise said as they made their way into the living room.

The super Chief

Peter Marshall was fed up of hanging around in the first class compartment of the Super Chief passenger train but getting some sleep was out of the question. Not that the first class compartment wasn't comfortable enough, it was perfect, but the excitement of the situation he was in just wouldn't let him rest.

The brand new luxury passenger train was the new flagship of the Atchison, Topeka and Santa Fe Railway and was later to be branded "The Train of the Stars" because of the Hollywood actors that used the train on a regular basis to travel between LA and Chicago. On this maiden journey however, there were hardly any first class passengers on board and although the train was very quiet, he hadn't slept much during the 36 hour journey from Chicago to LA. Now and then he had to look out of the window to assure himself that the train really was speeding across America and was amazed how quiet it was.

He checked the time on his wristwatch and then stood up, closed the buttons on his shadow stripe jacket and looked into the small mirror above the washbasin in his cabin. His muscular, unshaven, tanned face made him look more like a Chicago gangster than a scientist. He smiled, forming his right hand into a make-belief revolver and pretended to shoot his reflection in the mirror. Sniggering at his own childishness, he placed his flat cap onto his head with a slight tilt to one side, like he always did, opened the sliding door to his compartment and made his way outside. He walked along the corridor, past all the empty first class cabins and then through the diner car to the back of the train for what felt like the five hundredth time since leaving Chicago.

The fabrics of the upholstery, the wooden chairs and dining tables, even the perfectly set tables, gave him the feeling he was in a restaurant in Paris and not on a train speeding across America and everything had a wonderful smell of newness to it.

He spent a few minutes at the back of the train watching the flowers and trees rush by as the train sped toward it's destination. He watched almost hypnotized as they slowly floated off into the distance, seemingly getting slower and slower the further they got from the train to eventually become part of the distant horizon themselves. He thought for a while about what he was leaving behind and what the future had in store for him and was getting more and more excited the closer Super Chief got to LA. He made his way back into the diner car and sat down on one of the soft comfortable chairs, closed his eyes and laid back into the back of the seat and made sure he was alone before loosening his jacket buttons and shoes, something he would normally never do in public, but he had reached the stage where he was so tired that he couldn't care less what people thought of him. Relaxing to the rhythmic sound of the wheels rolling over the track and the gentle swinging of the diner car, he began to doze.

Although half asleep, he could still hear the rhythmic sound of the wheels racing over the track. D Dumm D Dumm D Dumm.......D Dumm D Dumm D Dumm.

The lady with a trolley containing drinks and snacks was doing one last run through the train to try and get a few more sells before the train reached its destination, came into the dining car and Peter realized straight away that something was different and was wide awake in an instant

"Oh I'm sorry sir, I didn't want to wake you up so rudely, just wanted to ask if jall want summ'n to eat or drink before we git t LA." the trolley lady said.

"No problems mam, how long is it before we arrive?" Peter asked.

"We will be arriving in about half an hour." She replied.

"Oh OK, than I'll have a packet of Ritz crackers and a Royal brown Cola please."

The lady served peter who gave her a dollar bill out of his wallet.

"Keep the change." Peter said smiling.

"You sure sir?" she asked, with a look of astonishment on her face.

"You had better move on before I change my mind." Peter said smiling to the lady.

"Well thank you sir and enjoy your time in LA." she said as she pushed the trolley into the empty first class compartment.

The first day in LA

The wheels of the train began to screech and the train seemed to be slowing down, Peter turned to look out of the window and could now see the City of LA and the ocean beyond. He was now more excited than ever about his move to California, the last time he felt this excited was when he moved to Oxford in England to begin his Studies.

After graduating out of the Oxford University Department of Physics in 1929, he had returned to Chicago to become part of the family business.

Oxford and Chicago couldn't have been more different and during his time in England he had often wondered if the two cities were on the same planet at all. The buildings, cars , People and countryside were nothing like his home town and he would rather have stayed on in England after graduation, but his father had insisted on his return to the States. The plan was set for him to become second in command of the company and Technical advisor to his father who was now one of the most well known architects in Chicago.

In the dawning of the age of the skyscraper, building companies needed three types of people working for them. Architects, scientists and lots of hard working men and the connection between architecture and Physics was becoming more important as ever before the skyscrapers becoming taller and more sophisticated as time went on. But five years working for family, especially his father had proved to Peter that doing his own thing was more cut out for him. Not that being second in command of a family business was a bad deal, it just wasn't challenging enough and slowly but surely, boredom was setting in and he needed a change.

He had taken up the job of writing a scientific column for the LA Times and the change of scenery would do him good.

Enough of sitting in an office with people he wouldn't spend five minutes of his free time with looking at plans of buildings and the fact that almost everyone in Chicago knew him as the rich kid, son of the star architect wasn't doing him any favours ether.

It didn't matter where he went, in town shopping, eating out at restaurants or just walking down the main street, he would be recognised, he was a celebrity in Chicago and he hated it.

Oxford and England had been much more relaxed and he missed the lifestyle he had lead as a student, he had pondered on the thought of moving back to England but made a compromise with his parents to stay in America although his Father wasn't too keen on his move away and him leaving the company. His father was against him doing anything by himself and had always held firmly onto the helm and had tried to steer him though life just as he wanted and what was best for the company,without considering Peter's wishes and needs.

"His image is important and we need to do everything right at exactly the right time." His father had said to his mother after Peter had said that he wanted to leave Chicago and the company business.

"To leave the company at such an important stage, what kind of message is that going to send to our customers?" his father had asked, but he knew that he day would come when Peter would leave anyway, the only open question was, when it would eventually happen.

LA was a long, long way from Chicago and what he was looking forward to most of all was walking through town without being recognised. Just becoming a normal person, leading a normal life.

What he didn't know at the time was, that his life would become less normal than he could have imagined.

He laid back into the seat hat was becoming more and more comfortable as the train picked up speed again and sped toward LA.

<u>Jenny Chandler</u>

The sound of the Super Chief braking and jolting as it pulled in to LA station awoke Peter from his doze. He sat upright in the seat, rubbed his eyes and yawned, waiting for the train to stop before he stood up and made his way to his compartment. After checking his suit and tie in the mirror and putting the tilt back onto his flat cap, he picked up his one suitcase and made his way outside, a quick look back just to make sure he hadn't left anything behind and then closed the sliding door of his compartment.

All of a sudden the train was full of people.

Teams of cleaning personnel trying to get onto the train, passengers trying to get off and the trolley lady all seemed to be getting in the way of each other and it reminded him of Chicago town centre on payday.

"Where the hell did all these people come from?" He asked himself.

He realised that he had been thinking out loud when the trolley lady answered and informed him that although the first class was almost empty, the second and working class compartments were full of passengers. And although his was the maiden journey of the Super Chief, it was more of a practice test run on the line from Chicago to LA, the official Maiden Journey would be three weeks later, full of celebrity's and press and the whole thing would be filmed for the cinema. Peter was glad to be on the train three weeks earlier and promised himself never to travel first class again.

"Maybe get more chance of meeting some interesting folk." he thought to himself and decided as he was leaving the Super Chief that from that point on his life would be different.

He stood on the platform floor, waved and smiled to the trolley lady, she was having problems getting passed a man who was doing his beast to sweep the floor between passengers trying to get off and workers trying to get onto the train.

The station wasn't as busy as he had thought it would be even for a Sunday morning and he made his way toward the main entrance. After finding a phone booth, he put his suitcase, on the floor between his feet and pulled a piece of paper out of his jacket pocket. He had written the phone number he was to ring in his arrival on the small piece of paper and put it into the pocket of the Jacket he would be wearing when he arrived. That way he couldn't lose important information that he would need at a later date.

Many years later a very clever person would invent the file o fax and much later the smart phone,making it much easier to remember important appointments or the name and number of the girl you had met the night before.

"LA Times Reception." A lady with a terrible squeaky voice answered the phone.

"Hello, it's Peter Marshall here." He answered.

"Ah so you have arrived safe and well, I will send your driver to pick you up, its a white Cadillac so he should be easy to notice." She said.

Peter hung up the phone, gathered his baggage and as he made his way to the pavement outside he heard the tooting of a car horn and he looked up to see the white Cadillac approaching, the driver waving frantically.

"Mr Marshall Sir." the driver shouted as he parked the car. "I'll put your things in the back sir, you take a seat, I'll be with you in a jiffy". The driver said, who seemed to be somewhat nervous as he came back to the front of the car.

"Err Mr Marshall Sir, passengers don't normally sit in the front seat." The driver said.

"A come on man, it's my first time in LA and I get a free sight seeing tour of the city and you want to banish me into the back seat." Peter winged like a small boy who had been told that he wasn't allowed an ice cream on a hot summers day.

"Sir, no problem really, I just ain't used to sitting next to passengers, you can sit where ever you want." Peter smiled.

"Oh and stop calling me Sir, please its Peter or Pete to you"

"Ah OK, well everyone just calls me Spike." The driver said.

"How long is the drive to my Hotel?" Peter asked.

"Only a few minutes, the Hotel, Station and the Times Building are all within a few minutes of each other." Spike replied and Peter laughed as Spike started the Cadillac and pulled out onto the road.

A short time later they pulled up in front of the Hotel. Spike took Peter's suitcase out of the car and handed it to a young black pageboy who nodded at Peter.

"Good day to you Sir." the page said, ushering Peter toward the reception and Spike closed the trunk of the Cadillac.

 "Will pick you up at two tomorrow." He said waving at Peter, who smiled back.

"Have a nice Sunday Spike, see you tomorrow."

A young woman smiled at Peter as he walked up to the reception desk.

"Mr Marshall sir, your suite is on the second floor, room 248, it is only temporary, you will be getting one of the penthouse suites as soon as they are refurbished." She said. Peter nodded, leaned over the reception and asked the lady something, lowering his voice and glancing at the pageboy. The reception lady answered, also lowering her voice so the page couldn't understand what she was saying. The page didn't seem to be all that bothered, it wasn't the first time a guest had asked that they only wanted to be served by white people and it probably wouldn't be the last time either. Peter made his way to the Elevator and the Page followed him,pushing a trolley with Peter's suitcase on top of it.

When they arrived the boy placed Peters suitcase in the main room of the suite, which consisted of a dining - living room, a bedroom that was not much bigger than the king size bed it was holding and the adjacent bathroom was just big enough for the Shower, bathtub and toilet. There was a large balcony and each room had windows that went from the ceiling all the way down to the floor, which gave you the feeling that the suite was much bigger than it really was.

The Page stood in the hallway of the suite, next to the main door and waited for the order from Peter to leave. Peter held a finger up in the air as if to say that he had forgotten something and took two dollars out of his wallet.

"Thanks very much for your help, where are you from Mr Haley?" He asked.

The Page stepped back with an astonished look on his face, wondering how Mr Marshall could know his name.

"I'm from South Carolina Sir."

"No man, I mean originally." Peter said, making a circular motion in front of his face with a finger.

"Oh, you mean because I'm Black, well originally my ancestors came from Africa Sir."

"Please stop calling me Sir, I ain't used to that, my real name is not Sir just as your real name is not Haley, you can call me Pete or Peter."

The Pageboy laughed. "Alex, my name is Alex" he said out loud. Don't know what my original African name is though , maybe in will find that out one day." Alex said.

"Ever thought about what you want to do later, I mean when you get older?" Peter asked.

"I would like to study, Journalism, maybe write a book." Alex replied.

"Well I am a journalist as of tomorrow and I haven't got a clue what it is going to be like, but I will keep you posted." Peter said smiling.

"And now git out ah mah room Alex Haley, yall wasted enough of mah precious time already." Peter said doing his best cotton field overseer impersonation.

"Yes sir Massa Peter sir, I'll be on my way fas as I can." Alex sniggered and replied, playing along with Peters impersonation. He stopped as he got to the door of Peters Suite.

"If you need anything, anything at all Peter, just let me know I will be happy to oblige." he said holding the two dollars in the air.

Peter nodded and smiled.

"Will do Alex." He said as Alex left his suite.

Peter waited a few minutes before he rung reception.

"Hi it's Peter Marshall here, thank you for letting me know what the pageboy's name is, I will skip lunch today, I really need a few hours sleep more than anything."

"Shall we give you a wake up call for dinner this evening." The girl asked.

"Yes that would be great." He said, as he loosened off his tie, he had already taken off his shoes and the bathtub was slowly filling up with hot water. He was so tired that he couldn't even remember getting out of the bath and going to bed and after what seemed like only a few minutes he heard a knock on the door to his bedroom. He sat up in bed and glanced at the clock on the wall. "Six Thirty." He mumbled to himself.

"Hello, who is it." He asked . The bedroom door opened slowly and a tall woman with a long yellow evening dress and long blonde hair entered the room.

"Hi I'm Jenny Chandler, I said to the reception that I would do your wake up call."

"Ah so you are Mr Chandlers.......?"

"Sister" Jenny butted in before he could finish the sentence and turned his back on her, sitting on the edge of his bed to pull his trousers on.

Jenny made her way to the balcony and Peter got dressed, ruffled his hair and checked his look in the mirror. Although he had slept soundly, he still looked quite tired and was looking forward to getting a good nights sleep. As he made his way through his suite to the balcony, he saw her standing lop sided, one hand in the balcony railing and the other holding a cigarette, pretending to look out over the city. The way she stood, she could have been a model for evening dresses and it looked like she had practised the pose for hours on end before coming to his suite.

"Hi." Peter said smiling as he entered the balcony. "I just slept all afternoon, probably eight hours but it only seemed like a few minutes, I was so tired."

"Damn long train journey from Chicago." Jenny nodded.

"So why are you doing my wake up call?" He asked.

"My brother told me to, I was actually supposed to be at a friends birthday party today, enjoying myself so I was pretty angry when he told me this morning that should have dinner with you today, said we should get to know each other socially before we start our professional relationship tomorrow." There was a pregnant pause and Jenny stubbed out her cigarette and shrugged her shoulders.

"But it's OK, he is right in saying that I suppose." she added.

"Ah so we will be working on the column together?" Peter asked, brushing an imaginary piece of fluff from her right shoulder. Jenny frowned at his fluff brushing action and then smiled. It wasn't often that someone did that kind of thing, most of the men she knew were work colleagues and men in general kept a safe distance from her when they realised who she was, probably thinking that it would be bad for their ego to be in a relationship with such a powerful woman and one of the top chiefs at the LA Times.

"Working together.... well sort of, I am your new boss." She answered.

"Sorry you had to miss the party." Peter then mentioned, looking out across the city as if he was trying to spot something.

"That's no problem Peter, your better looking that he will ever be anyway." She winked and they both laughed out loud.

"I'm starving." peter said and held his hand out to Jenny. "My Lady." He said smiling. She smiled back at him, laid her hand on his and they made their way to the restaurant.

Peters mouth fell wide open as they entered the restaurant and Jenny looked at him and laughed.

"You have been in a restaurant before haven't you?" she asked.

"Yes I have, but nothing like this, all this marble, gold and leather,and the buffet just looks delicious." He answered.

Peter's stomach was reminding him on a regular basis that he had chosen to miss the midday meal. The Ritz Crackers had filled a small gap but weren't enough to keep him going all day and it was high time he got something to eat.

A waiter nodded to a table that had been reserved for them.

"I will bring the wine." he said in the poshest English accent Peter had ever heard and he watched the waiter with raised eyebrows as he seemed to float off toward the kitchen.

"Lets get the business side of things done so we can sit back and enjoy the rest of the evening." Jenny said as they sat down .

"Have you thought about how you will start your page in the paper?" She asked.

"I have made a few thoughts, how often will my Page be in the paper?" He asked.

Jenny hated it when her questions weren't answered and the worse thing of all was when somebody threw a question right back at her and she frowned at him to let him know she was pissed off.

"Four times per month, in the Sunday edition."

"Oh OK, and have you thought about how much I will be paid?" Peter asked.

She poured them both a glass of water and smiled, trying to cause a pregnant pause in the question and answering game that was going on between them. He was beginning to control the conversation and that wasn't good for business. But she was beginning to like him, he was a real man who knew exactly what he wanted and needed and she was sure he knew how to get it, and he was on hell of a sexy son of a bitch. She thought and felt a funny feeling in her stomach as she caught him watching her pouring the water into his glas.

"He's controlling me, he is not only controlling the conversation, he is actually controlling me!" Jenny thought to herself. "And it feels wonderful." She thought and smiled.

"I have to get back in charge of this, or he will bite bits off me, chew them like a baseball player chews tobacco and spit them out until there is nothing left of me." She Thought.

"Your write up will cover the complete third page. I want you to write about new interesting inventions,

Auto mobiles and of course the new and modern buildings in Los Aneles." Jenny said full of enthusiasm and Peter nodded in agreement, then looked her straight in the eye with his eyebrows raised and his head tilted to one side as if to say.

"Stop beating about the bush girl and answer my question".

There it was again, that funny feeling, this time it went from her stomach and shot down her legs, and she was glad she was sitting down, if she was stood up she would have probably fallen over, just as she had fallen in love with Peter.

"Pick yourself up Jenny chandler, get control of yourself or this sexy son of a gun is going to take you to pieces." She thought to herself, trying her best to regain her composure.

"One hundred dollars." Jenny said nervously.

"I mean a hundred dollars, Ok that will do for starters but I was expecting a bit more than that from such an established company like yours." Peter replied after taking a sip of water.

Jenny lit up cigarette and looked around the restaurant, pretending that other people in the room were more important that Peter was, she smiled at the barkeeper as though she had known him all her life and he smiled back in the same way. She was trying to slow down the situation and get a grip of herself. Manipulating the situation was one of her favourite games but today she was up against probably one of the best in that game and Peter wondered if she always went though life as if she was acting some part on the silver screen, Jenny turned back to look at peter and tried her best to look disappointed at Peter's reaction.

"C'mon Mr Marshall, a hundred bucks a week plus hotel and all you can eat and drink, travel costs will be paid out double to make sure everything is covered, I think that sounds like a pretty good deal." Jenny said.

Peter pretended to look positively surprised.

"Four hundred a month plus all costs, yeah, now that is what I call a good deal." Peter smiled and rubbed his hands together and Jenny let out a sigh of relief.

Peter knew that he would be travelling quite a lot and with food and accommodation being covered, he could probably live quite well without really having to spend much of his wages.

The USA was still recovering from the depression caused by the Wall Street Crash in 1929 but it looked like 1935 would be the year to turn things around and the deal was more than acceptable, he knew that and was already planing to invest the four hundred dollars wage in Land and assets around LA. He also knew he would not work at the Times all his life and would probably need financial back up for any business ventures in the future. Peter asked Jenny if it was her idea to have a scientific third page.

"My brother had the idea some time ago, we had a kind of advertisement page where companies could show their new products, but it didn't hit off, most of the ads were not well written and it just wasn't entertaining enough. So we decided to change it to a kind of informative entertainment page, with pictures, graphs and interviews, information about all sorts of new interesting stuff. Just one product per week will be written about." Jenny took a sip of her wine.

"Almost every product on the market, be it, Cars Buildings, gadgets for the house and garden and even sports equipment, are all very interesting and in one way or another, either the product itself or the production process have something to do with physics." she said and sat back in her chair, smiling.

Peter knew that someone else had told her to say that and she had practised the sentence until it was perfect.

He also knew she didn't have a clue about physics.

"Sir, Mam, you can get your starters at the buffet and when I see you are ready I will serve the main course." The waiter said, as he floated past their table.

"I declare the business side of things done, lets eat!" Peter said, and they made their way to the buffet.

The Times

Peter was wide awake the following morning at six o'clock. The sleep the day before and the five hour sleep in the night had done him the world of good.

He got up and went into the dining room of his suite. On the table was a note from Jenny.

"See you at two in my office."

No mention about the evening and night they had spent together. After the meal they had ordered another bottle of wine and talked, laughed and got to know each other socially, much more than Jenny's brother had anticipated.

The waiter eventually kicked them out of the Restaurant and Jenny escorted Peter to the elevator. As he waited for the elevator, Jenny smiled and moved slightly so that their hands touched. Peter didn't seem to withdraw his hand and she knew he wanted her as much as she wanted him. As the elevator door opened and she saw that no one else was inside, she pushed him in, pressed the second floor button and began to kiss his face, lips and neck wildly. He held her shoulders and pushed her away with a serous look on his face, she shrugged her shoulders with a disappointed look on her face as if to ask if she had done something wrong.

Then he smiled and she flung her arms around his neck as the elevator stopped at the second floor.

Their first night together wasn't like two lovers making out for the first time, It was more like two people satisfying their needs. It was the best Sex he had ever experienced and Jenny took her "wild and risk taking" character to bed with her, which he fully enjoyed being part of but he wasn't sure if it was just a one off thing or if it would happen in a regular basis. He was hoping for the second option as he took the note and placed it in his bedside drawer.

After a few years the drawer would be full of small notes form Jenny.

He though about the evening before and the night he had spent with Jenny. He liked her, she was funny,interesting and a pleasant person to be with, OK she smoked too much and she wasn't the kind of woman he would marry and spend his whole life with, but a friendship with a small bonus when the lights went out appealed to him and he was more than happy with the start he had made in LA.

After breakfast he had a shower and shave and got dressed. After having another coffee he made his way outside to have a look around the area. He was a bit disappointed when he realised that LA was similar to all cities in the States he had been to, and what he had seen in pictures and films was an illusion,made to look good for the silver screen.

"Maybe I just expect too much." He thought as he returned to the Hotel.

He sat on one of the chairs in the lobby and ordered a coffee and an LA Times

"Amazing, you open the paper and the first thing you see is my page, this is the springboard I needed to jump to better things." He thought.

"Mr Marshall, is everything OK?" he heard a woman's voice asking, and realized that he probably had a huge smile on his face, like a teenager who had just had their first, bubble gum tasting, soft moist French kiss.

He Lowered the paper as the waitress asked if she could clear his cup and saucer away.

He looked up, "Oh everything's fine, I was just daydreaming." He said, and got up from the chair.

"Lunch will be served in your suite in half an hour." the waitress said.

"OK, thank you very much." He said, making his way to the elevator.

After lunch he was picked up by Spike in the white Cadillac and driven to the newly built LA Times Building, which was a statement of power and success in a time when America was just getting back on it's feet after the Wall Street Crash. Jenny's office was huge, with oak panelling on the walls,

Persian carpets, dark wood asian furniture and the rest was steel and leather. Peter wondered if LA and the Times had been part of the recession at all when there was a knock at the door and Bill Chandler walked in smiling.

"Peter I have heard so much about you, I'm so exited to greet you to LA and the Times." He said shaking Peters hand.

"Thank you very much." Peter said smiling.

"Jenny will be here in a few minutes, lets talk about the company you are now part of until she gets here." Bill added, turning to point at the portrait photographs hanging on the wall behind Jenny;s desk.

 "Harrisson Otis, who made the paper what it is today, also made our father general manager of the company. Before that our father was working in the fruit fields near LA and decided to go self employed, he invested all the money he had saved up, bought a Horse and cart and began a fruit delivery service. After a while he had the idea of adding the LA Times as one of his products and it didn't take long before he was one of the main purchasers of the paper. One day Harrison was checking though the sales statistics and questioned the sales office, why one person ordered so many copies of the Times and when he found out about dad's business he invited him in for a chat, within a few minutes they were more or less best buddys and a short time after that dad was managing director.. and the rest, as they say is history.

"Amazing how that all developed." Peter said, nodding at the portraits on the wall as Jenny walked into the office. Her smile turned into a frown of disappointment and she pointed at the huge desk.

"No coffee? You are starting to slacken off little brother I must say." she said trying to sound as cross as she could.

"She's my boss too." Bill said as he picked up the phone and politely ordered coffee for three in Jennys office.

"These are good people, who understand what it means to have to work hard for their money" Peter thought. "They had probably been told time and time again by their father, never to forget who you are and where you came from. Their father had come from one of the lowest classes and worst paid jobs, harvesting Fruit, to become the managing director of probably the most established company in LA."

He had hated the rich kids of Chicago who had no respect for the hard working people and had now and then had deliberateley organised meetings on building sites and not in his warm office. His father had once asked him why.

*"**The upper class should never forget that it is the working class people who pave the side walks under the red carpets they walk upon, build the houses they live in and hold up the pillars of the platforms they stand high upon, when the upper class lose that connection,they are doomed to failure**."* Peter had said.

It was the last time that his father questioned any of his actions and although Peter never had to do a days hard work in his life, he always respected the working class people for what they achieve.

The Meeting in Jenny's office was short. They spoke about the layout of the page,he was assigned a photographer and an assistant who would work together with him on the page they also agreed that Peter could work from his suite in the Hotel and organised everything he would need.

His Photographer, Rico, was a funny Italian man from the Bronx in New York and his Assistant a nice elderly lady called Mandy, who always wore the same cardigan and smelled like chocolate biscuits.

The three were a perfect team and after the first six months and write ups on the newest cars on the market, the first canned beer, the ballpoint pen and first freeze dry coffee were a huge success, Peter was given a pay rise of 100% and a 10% cut from the money the companies paid to get onto page three of the Times. Mandy and Rico also had very good ideas what to write about, Mandy being more interested in the newest gadgets for the house and Rico was the cars and sports fanatic. And with Photos, technical information and graphs, the page was always interesting and perfect for the working class reader, written in the language they understood. This was very important for Peter, and for business, as he was becoming better known in California and sooner or later his big opportunity as a scientist in one of the big companies would come. Sometimes he would be envious of the people he interviewed who had Jobs quality testing or developing products, but he was patient knowing that there was a right time for everything.

His time would come sure enough, he would become a scientist, developing a very important product. A Product that he would never have thought he would have anything to do with, not even in his wildest dreams.

The first day of war

The years up until 1939 were the most successful financial years Peter would ever have after leaving Chicago. The third page in the LA times was more successful than anyone could have imagined. It was a situation where there were no losers. The times sold more papers on Sundays than ever before, company's received a perfect, entertaining advertisement for up and coming products and Peter built up his reputation as a scientist and journalist. With plenty of free time he was able to build up a contact network of business people and scientists and also spent some of his free time building up a real estate company of his own, buying land in and around LA. He enjoyed working with his perfect team and although she was not the perfect partner for him, enjoyed his relationship with Jenny. Both Jenny and Peter knew that it wouldn't go on forever and that one day either Jenny or Peter would fall in love with someone else and their, "Easy like Sunday morning" friendship would some to an end. Both accepted the fact and were happy just to spend some time together now and then in Peter's Suite, go to partys together or enjoy a ride out into the countryside.

Jenny would be the first one to fall in love.

It seemed that everything was just perfect for Peter, Jenny and the Times, in late 1938 however, the winds blowing around the world began whispering messages of change. Changes that would cause the world to be a more hostile and dangerous place and it would never be the same again. Changes that would effect his relationship with Jenny more than either of them would have thought.

Japan was already at war again with China and the fact that war in Europe was more or less imminent caused the general public in the USA to be more interested in things that were going on elsewhere than the physics of newest products in the market. Jenny, Bill and Peter decided to scale down the write ups to one a month, a decision that Peter was quite happy with as his real estate business was booming, the first Land plots had been built on and he was cashing in on rent and lease more and more each month. Money he re invested into his business, living in the same suite since his arrival in LA, hardly spending any of his money that he earned at the Times, the scientist Network he had set up had begun to be involved in the production of different products all over the USA and the future seemed to be going in the direction he had hoped for when he left Chicago in 1935.

This all would change in late August 1939

Peter was visiting Muroc air base where he owned land. The base commander had contacted Peter and informed him that the current political situation world wide had prompted the US military to build up its defence capabilities. Many Aircraft were obsolete and a huge project to develop new Planes and equipment would be starting in early 1940. the Muroc Air base was to be extended and used as one of the main test sites for new equipment and the land that Peter owned at the end of one of the runways would be required.

Peter travelled to the base on the 1 of September 1939 and agreed on deal that the US Government would rent the land that Peter owned. The meeting only took about half an hour, the Base commander then gave Peter a guided tour of the base, explaining all the changes that would be made before they went to the officers mess for dinner.

During dinner they heard someone in the Kitchen shouting.

"Jesus they have gone and done it for real!"

A Radio was turned up loud and they heard a reporter announce.

"Ladies and Gentlemen, we have received information from NBC that the German Armed forces have invaded Poland. We will keep you informed with NEWS as the day goes on"

"Do you think we will go to war" Peter asked the commander.

"No, I don't think we will go to war Peter, I know we will. It's just a question of time."

Peter nodded in agreement, a grim look on his face.

"I don't think any fighting will be done here on American soil, but it will change our lives forever." the commander added.

Both the commander and Peter didn't say a word for a few minutes.

"It's the outcome I am afraid of." The commander said.

Peter frowned and shrugged his shoulders.

"The world will never be the same after today Peter, you mark my words."

Peter stayed overnight in the officers mess and made his way back to LA after breakfast.

He began to follow the political situation and development of the War in Europe and in the Far East and even thought about developing military Equipment to better the safety and comfort of soldiers in the field. He secretly hoped however, that the War would soon be over and that a peaceful solution would be found.

On the 7th of December 1941 his hopes would be crushed into oblivion and his life changed forever.

It was the day of the attack on Pearl Harbour and the day America went to War.

He was sitting in his hotel suite, staring out of the window thinking about the global situation when he heard the NEWS on the radio. Up until this moment the War had seemed so far away, and although LA was a long way from Pearl Harbour it now felt like it was all happening right outside his hotel. Japanese bombs had been dropped on American soil and the second world war had struck home. There was a frantic knock on the door and Jenny rushed in.

"Peter, have you heard the NEWS!" She cried.

Peter nodded without saying a word, a grim look on his face.

I don't care what happens, you will not go to war. I refuse to lose my best friend...say you wont go Peter..please." tears were now rolling down her face.

Peter nodded again.

"I have received some information about different scientific projects that aid the War effort, developing equipment and weapons, if I accept, I will be assigned to one of the projects and can stay in America as a civilian." he said.

"Please accept, Peter....please." Jeny was now sobbing uncontrollably at the thought of losing her best, and only real friend.

Peter wiped the tears from her face. "I already have my sweetheart" He said.

That day they made love for the first time since meeting in 1935

The day the Japanese attacked Pearl Harbour would change many things. One of these was the fear in the back of peoples minds world wide, a fear that it was possible that every civilian world wide could be directly effected by war.

In the later stages of the second world war it would become a chilling reality that the civilian working class population and their homes, would become the target of strategic bombing.

Peter and Jenny had sex on numerous occasions since 1935 but on that day in December 1941 they became lovers.

The following weeks they spent almost every moment they could together. Sitting on the balcony of Peters hotel Suite, Drinking wine until late at night before making love until the first rays of sunlight changed the colour of the buildings of LA and then sleeping until midday.

Peter was assigned to a Project near San Francisco to develop a surveillance Plane and left LA forever a few days before Christmas 1941.

On the day he left, Jenny and Peter had lunch in the Hotel Restaurant together with Spike, Rico, Mandy and Alex Haley. After the lunch Peter wished his team and Alex who he had become good friends with, all well and took Jenny by the hand. They walked to the elevator without saying a word. Jenny smiled at Peter.

"Remember that first night in 1935?"

"Oh yes, during lunch I thought that we are either going to scratch each others eyes out or end up in bed together."

Jenny laughed out loud as the elevator doors opened and the walked inside.

Once in his suite Peter told her that he had written a will, leaving all his assets and money to Jenny, just in case anything happened to him.

"You're only going to be in a small base near San Francisco and not in Europe or the Far East where it's dangerous." Jenny said frowning.

"Or have you made plans I don't know about?"

"It's just in case babe, just in case." He said as he looked at the open suitcase next to his bed.

"Better start packing then." He said, taking Jenny in his arms and kissing her softly on the cheek.

"I will travel down to LA as often as I can and we can write, and call every day....." Jenny held a finger on his mouth and shook her head.

"We can't plan or promise anything my love, not in this situation, just take care of yourself as best you can and lets hope for the best." She said.

Peter knew that their relationship would not stand the test of time and space, their friendship would go on forever but their love affair would be over the moment he left LA.

"He held her in his arms, you look after yourself too, ok."

Jenny nodded and let go of his hand as she made her way to the door.

Hey both knew that it was over before it had begun, what they didn't know was that Jenny was carrying his baby.

San Joakin Valley

Later that same evening he was picked u by a US Army staff car and driven though the night to his new home, the officers mess of a small army air base in San Joakin Valley not far from San Fransisco.

He hardly got any sleep during the journey and it reminded him of the journey from Chicago to LA in the Super Chief all those years ago. Excited about the project and new people he would be meeting. He thought about his time in England, studying in Oxford, the years he had worked together with his father and that he never thought, being a pacifist and against violence in any form, that he would, one day be involved in a military project. He also thought about his Time in LA, his relationship with Jenny and friendship with Bill Chandler and Alex Haley.

About Spike, who had joined the Navy and would sadly lose his life in the fierce fighting in the battle of Iwo Jama in 1945, about the lovely Reception girl, who he had secretley fallen in love with, who would lose her husband when he would fall, fighting on Ohama Beach during the D Day attacks.

He thought about the base commander at Muroc and what he had said about the war, and what could happen after it eventually came to an end. The thoughts about how the world would change scared him more than the war itself, but he did as Jenny had said and hoped for the best.

He was torn away from his thoughts when the driver slowed the staff car, stopped and opened his window.

"Password, six six two three" he said to the armed guard who then nodded and opened the red and white barrier to let them into the base.

He driver dropped him off in front of the officers mess where he was greeted by an English army Captain who was the military officer assigned to oversee the project he would be working on.

The driver placed his suitcase on the pavement next to Peter, saluted the Captain and drove off to get some well earned sleep.

Although it was only 5 o'clock in the morning it was much brighter outside than in the back of the staff car and he had to squint his eyes to be able to see properly as he smiled and nodded at the Army Captain, who was squinting at peter in the same way as if trying to read something that was printed on his forehead.

"Bloody hell if it isn't Peter Marshall himself" the Captain bellowed out, almost frightening Peter to death.

Peter looked the officer in the face, trying to recognise who this person with the extremely loud voice, was. The Captain took off his army hat to reveal a pathetic looking long curly fringe that resembled a mop stuck to his forehead. The outragious fringe was emphasized by a very short back and sides.

"Well I'll be damned, Jimmy Blythe." Said Peter, who was now smiling from cheek to cheek.

"You are looking in good shape Peter old bean, are you still rowing?" Jimmy asked.

"Unfortunately not, but I have been able to stay in shape, in had a great job the last six years with plenty of free time."

Jimmy Blythe was in the Cambridge rowing team at the same time Peter rowed for Oxford and although they were sporting rivals at the time, they had liked each other and had kept in touch while Peter was in England, but lost contact when Peter left for the States.

"Come on then, I'll show you your accommodation and you can get some sleep, after lunch I will show you around this loveley place." Jimmy said, putting his hat back on and waving his arms around in excitement.

"Sounds like a good plan Sir, or do in have to call you Captain Blythe?" Peter asked.

"Well you can cut that out straight away, it's Jim or Jimmy to you, I am actually very seldom in Uniform anyway, only when some top knob military personnel come to visit and on the queens official birthday." Jimmy said smiling.

He showed Peter his room in the mess, which was different to his suite in LA, the bedroom was a little bigger and there was no balcony and no Bath or shower. The bathroom was a few doors down the corridor and next to Peters room was a small kitchen where he could cook snacks and make coffee or tea.

"Ok, you get some kip then and I will come and pick you up at about thirteen hundred hours." Jimmy said as he left Peters room.

Peter lay on his bed and listened to Jimmy's footsteps as he made his way down the hallway, he then looked at a calender on the wall opposite his bed.

"In three days it will be Christmas, doesn't feel like Christmas at all." he thought out loud to himself as he looked out of the window to see that the new day was slowly dawning, he could now make out the trees in the garden of the officers mess, swaying in the remarkably warm breeze for California at this time of year and he could hear women's voices talking and laughing somewhere outside and the birds were starting to sing.

"It definitely doesn't feel like Christmas, he thought as he fell into a peaceful, dreamless sleep.

Project Vought Kingfisher

"Wakey wakey, rise and shine, come on, stand by your bed!" Jimmy Blythe shouted as he burst into Peters room without knocking. Peter yawned, rubbed his eyes and looked at Jimmy with raised eyebrows.

"Man I'm starving, what time is it?" he asked.

"Seven O'clock." Answered Jimmy.

"Aw Jimmy, I thought you wanted to wake me up earlier, I could have starved to death here I in my sleep." Peter winged.

"Well you know what it's like Peter, things to do, people to see and before you know it you are an old man living in a home on the south coast of England and can't remember a thing about your life, or in this case you missed an appointment to wake up your new colleague." Jimmy said, walking back and forth in front of the Peters bedroom window like a lion in a zoo cage, hoping that it will be able to get out of the dreadful situation it is by walking back and forth all day. Eventually he stopped walking and stood for a few seconds, looking out of the Window. He could feel Peter watching him and eventually turned to face Peter and raised his hands in surrender.

"Okay, okay, to be honest I forgot all about you, but I've ordered us an nice supper in the mess restaurant to make amends, which will be served in approximately." Jimmy pretended to look at a watch on his wrist.

"Well right about now really."

He never wore a watch and explained to Peter on the way to supper that it was a great way to chat up ladies.

"*Excuse me, could you tell me what time it is please.*" He pretended to ask somebody as he explained Peter how he used the trick.

"Then they look at their watch and I say"

"*Good heavens, those are the most beautiful hands I have ever set m eyes on.*" And when they fall for it, you will be enjoying a Champaign breakfast after a stormy night between the sheets."

"And when they don't fall for it." Peter asked.

"Ah, then I say something like". *Well it wasn't your hands I was talking about my dear but the ones on your wristwatch.*"

That way I can unload and make the situation safe without hurting anybody's feelings."

Peter Smiled, nodded and wondered if Jimmy was a virgin. They sat for a while in the mess after supper and talked about their time at University, different Cities they had been to, girls and sport. Peter liked Jimmy, he hadn't got to know him all that well back in the twenties but he was funny and charming and Peter found him easy to get on with.

They also had a few things in common and although Jimmy was an Army captain and they both worked on the same Military project, they were totally and utterly against the war and any violence what so ever.

"So how did you end up here in California and not in some field in Europe, freezing your balls off?" Peter asked.

"Well I have actually been here since 1939 working on different aviation projects that both the US and UK Military have set up together and someone back in England decided that when the war started I would be more use as a scientist that a combat soldier. It makes more sense for me to be here and I would be as much use as a chocolate fireguard in hell in a battlefield situation." Jimmy explained.

"And who was this someone who made that decision?" Peter winked at Jimmy who looked shyly toward the floor as if checking his shoelaces.

"Well actually it was my father. He always knew I was against violence and fighting and the only reason I became a soldier was because he insisted on it, family tradition and all that nonsense. When I told him I wanted to become an army padre he just told me to stop being silly and made sure I was posted to his regiment so he could take care of me and began straight away to look for a posting for me where I would be far away from any fighting."

"Good man your father." Peter commented.

"Yes he is, he regretted insisting that I become a soldier and wanted to protect me as best he could, I just hope to god he gets through this bloody war alright."

"Isn't he retired now?" asked Peter.

"Yes he is, but knowing him he will be up for a fight as soon as he gets the chance, I told my mother to lock him in the garden shed and let him out when the whole thing is over.... right, now we know why I am here and not on the western front making a fool of myself, lets talk about the Project you will be working on." Jimmy said obviously wanting to change the subject fast and Peter sat up in his chair, his face full of anticipation.

"At ease Peter, it's not all that exciting, to be honest the most interesting thing about it is the name.... Operation Vought Kingfisher." Jimmy said, trying to be as dramatic as he could, almost spilling his coffee as the waved his arms around, pretending to be a air-plane.

Peter sniggered at Jimmy's actions.

"Well it definitely sounds interesting that's for sure."
He said.

"Yes the Vought kingfisher is a surveillance plane
that also can be used for air sea rescue, i have started
developing a catapult and crane system which can be
mounted onto small ships, that way the aircraft can
be launched from the ship and because it has a float
and wheel undercarriage it can land on water and be
picked up by the crane and put back on board after
each mission. The whole thing doesn't take up too
much space and the catapult and Plane are less than
thirty meters long. So the "Dove" can be bought into
action by very small, fast boats." Jimmy explained
proudly.

"It's very interesting stuff, why do you call it the
Dove?" Peter asked.

"Ah, the dove thing, well last year I was watching
birds fly around this place and noticed that when
they take off, from the roof of a building for
example, they lose a bit of height and once they get
going they gain height again, a kind of dip down,
rise up motion, the Plane does that too when it is
launched from the catapult."

Peter wondered if he had ever seen a dove doing
that, or any other bird for that matter and decided to
himself that it was probably another in of Jimmy s
stories for chatting up the ladies.

"Up until now the plane has been used in Air Sea rescue and Anti Submarine operations but the long range reconnaissance version that we will be developing will only be 4 tons in weight and not the normal operational 6 tons." Jimmy explained.

"Sounds like most of the work has been done." Peter commented.

"Well you are more or less right in saying that, but at the moment the Plane is mostly launched by aircraft carriers, which means that it is not all that flexible or independent, which it needs to be to be able to carry out reconnaissance work. We have used a modified Motor torpedo boat, that was acceptable but we need to reduce the weight of the Plane and boat to increase the speed and range, I have an idea to use the British MTB 102, it is only 21 Meters in length, the catapult is 20 meters so it fits perfectly onto the boat. So the plane will be more or less parked on top the the boat and can be launched at any time. The crane is fixed to the stern of the boat which is scrapped of all weapons to make it lighter, two extra external fuel tanks will be fitted to both sides of the hull which look a bit like torpedoes, giving the vessel a range that makes it possible to get from the USA to Japan and back and the pacific crossing takes about 10 Days. The project will take a few years to complete, I hope the war will be over much earlier but this project is well ahead of it's time and will be used by the military in decades to come." Jimmy sat back in his chair with a satisfied look on his face.

"But if all the scinetific development work has been done, where do I come into this?" Peter asked.

"Well Peter, I have decided that you will be the test pilot." Jimmy smiled and winked at Peter, rubbing his hands together as if trying to warm himself up.

Peter raised his eyebrows.

"Me, the test Pilot, only thing I ever flown was a kite when I was a kid and that crash landed most of the time." Peter commented.

Jimmy laughed out loud.

"Well you had better buck your ideas up for this one Peter my old bean, if you crash this kite on a regular basis it could get a bit expensive in the long run."

Peter stared at Jimmy with a look of shock on his face and wondered why the cost of the project would be more important that the well being of his new friend and colleague.

Jimmy took a gulp of his coffee, sniggering at his own comment.

"Only joking Peter, it's not that expensive and you will have a parachute as well." Jimmy burst into laughter as he buttered another piece of toast.

Although now smiling too, Peter still had a look on shock in his eyes, Jimmy laid his toast on his plate and looked Peter in the eyes.

"Peter, you don't think for one minute that I would chose you for this project if I knew it would be dangerous do you."

"Ah, so you chose me for the project?" Peter asked.

"Yes I did, there were 15 scientists to chose from and I looked for someone who I would have a bit in common with." Jimmy said quietly.

Peter frowned as if to ask Jimmy what the hell the two of them had in common.

"OK, we were in England studying at the same time, we are both scientists and in the rowing team of our University...we are both quite muscular, well you are a bit more than me, but I'm working on that one.....

Peter held up a hand to signal Jimmy to stop talking.

"Stop beating around the bush Jimmy why did you chose me for this project?"

Jimmy took a bite of his toast leant forward and lowered his voice.

"Remember the boat race in 1925?" he asked.

"How could I forget, our boat sank." Peter smiled.

"Yes that was a shame, but do you remember the after race party.?

"Yes I do, very fond memories." Peter said.

"We talked a bit about the first world war and that we are both pacifists and that we would never take up weapons and fight, do you remember?" Jimmy asked, now almost whispering.

"Yes I remember that too." Peter answered.

"The Dove and the vessel it will be mounted on, will carry no weapons, it is not a fighting vessel but surveillance and sea rescue equipment, I needed someone who hates war and fighting as much as I do to work on this one with me." Jimmy said.

"We will help pilots and sailors who have been shot down or sunk, to get back to safety, all of them Peter, no matter what side they are fighting on, Because ant the end of the day Peter, nobody on this planet wants to go to war, I am sure of that."

"So what was all that about this morning, not being able to recognise me and all that?" Peter asked

"Well, this morning I didn't know that we were going to have this conversation, and nobody is allowed to know the real reason I chose you, you are actually not suitable for the job at all, you have had nothing to do with aviation or any military equipment for that matter so it was a good job that nobody will find out why I chose you. Two pacifists on one project is not good for the military my friend and walls have ears, so it would be better if we never talk about this again." Jimmy whispered.

It was the first time since getting to the base that

Peter had experienced Jimmy being serious and he liked the funny, much too loud and sometimes ridiculously predicable Jimmy much better. Needing to change the subject, Peter shoved his plate to one side and poured himself another coffee.

"Why don't you want to be the pilot?" He asked.

"To be honest with you Peter, I couldn't think of a better job for me, would definitely be a great way of getting the ladies swooning around me all day." Jimmy said smiling.

Peter Smiled back at him. "He's a virgin, one hundred percent." He thought to himself.

"The Problem is that I'm absolutely terrified of heights." Jimmy confessed.

"So for the next six months I will be getting the whole system ready for the first tests while you learn to fly the Dove." Jimmy explained and watched Peters face for some kind of reaction.

Peter just nodded.

"Sounds like a good plan to me, I'm in on it." He said.

The following six months were very intense and busy, Jimmy and Peter hardly saw each other. Jimmy spent a lot of time in San Francisco Bay setting up the boat while Peter carried out a crash Pilots course.

Most Army Air Corps pilots during the second world war carried out a pre flight course which was broken down into two phases, the first Phase, a testing Physical fitness and military training course, followed by a classroom phase in Physics and Maths and for those who would be piloting the Kingfishger, a special flight training in a Kingfisher simulator called "The bluebox" and then finally, flight training in the aircraft itself.

As Peter would not be carrying out any combat operations, he didn't absolve the pre flight training and most of his flight training was based on the catapult take off and sea landing of the plane.

Jimmy was in San Francisco on the day Peter got back to the base and the following morning Peter was sat alone in the mess having breakfast when he received a hard pat on the back and almost chocked, still coughing he turned around.

"Jimmy, hey how are you getting on my friend." Peter bellowed, doing his best impression of his friend that he could.

Jimmy smiled. "Glad to have you back on board my friend." He said and sat down opposite Peter.

"Unfortunately I have some bad NEWS." He said.

Peter sat up in his chair frowning.

"The military have decided that the new version will not be required until after the war and our new assignment is to train pilots here at the base who will be using the actual system, we are to modify the current plane and boat to get the best system possible and just optimize as we go along."

"Man that is bad NEWS." Peter said.

"Now the good NEWS." Jimmy said rubbing his hands together, Peter smiled and rolled his eyes.

"I've built one anyway, the prototype ship is ready and fitted with the extra fuel tanks, crane and launch catapult, ready to go,the only thing that is missing is the plane."

Peter was still frowning. "OK, but if the military don't need it, why build it? He asked.

"Peter, we don't know how this war is going to develop, it is possible that we my have to get away from here as fast as we can and the boat is perfect for that. Fast, small and more or less invisible to RADAR and you will have to be damned lucky to spot it at sea with the naked eye. The vessel is hidden in an old boat shed in Tomalas bay jut north of San Fransisco."

Peter nodded.

"I propose that we drive up there twice a week and fill the thing up with fuel and rations so that if we need to get away from this place, we can live on the boat for a long time, maybe we will never need it but you never know what the future has in store."

"Sounds like a good plan" Peter said.

They spent most of the following two years training pilot to use the kingfisher and seamen to use the vessel and gathered reports from combat missions to make modifications as the war carried on.

In spring 1945, the war in Europe was coming to an end but in the Pacific a final huge attack on Japan was being planned. An invasion of Japan where almost all of the available US Navy and Marine Corps and allied military forces would be involved. It was a tense time where everyone was hoping for the best, but expecting the worst.

On a warm and sunny July morning, Peter and Jimmy were sat in the mess after breakfast, when a man dressed in the official Cambridge rowing team trousers and jumper came into the room looking very nervous, as if he needed to find someone fast.

<u>Crispin</u>

"Bloody hell it's CHD, where the dickens have you been man! Haven't you heard there's a war on?" Jimmy bellowed, winking at Peter and the very suspicious man rushed to their table and sat down next to Jimmy.

"Jim, thank God I have found you." He said. "I have been involved in a project at Los Alamos, it's not good my friend, I needed to talk to you about it." the man said looking nervously at Peter.

"Ah, this is Peter Marshall, a very good friend of mine and my partner in crime during this bloody war. Peter please let me introduce my friend Crispin Heathcote Drummond, whom we call CHD, because it it easier to say and makes a better impression on the ladies." Jimmy said.

Peter and Crispin nodded to each other and Crispin let out a sigh of relief.

"So what is all this Los Alamos thingy you are so worried about?" Jimmy asked, looking across the table and nodding slightly at Peter who winked back.

"Is there any where we can go to talk about it, it really is sensitive stuff?" Crispin whispered.

"In the hangar where the Planes are parked, we have a small office where only Peter and I have access." Jimmy said, the three stood up from the table and made their way directly to the hangar.

"Do you have a camera here, I have a roll of film I want to show you?" Crispin asked as they opened the huge rolling door of the hangar.

Peter confirmed that they had a camera and projector they used for the pilots courses and Jimmy and Peter waited patiently as Crispin set up everything to show them the film he had brought with him, he nodded to Jimmy to signal that he was ready and Peter turned the lights off and closed the curtains of the only window in the office.

The film started...

Typical Walt Disney music sounded out of the speaker and the "Three caballeros" a Walt Disney film from 1944 started up on the screen.

Both Jimmy and Peter began to snigger and Crispin knocked on the table to regain their attention and as they both looked up, the Disney film stopped abruptly and the screen turned white, the words

"The Manhattan Project, Trinity test"

showed up in large black writing.

For the next ten minutes both Peter and Jimmy just stared at the screen in silence and as the film was over the only words were Jimmy saying.

"Good lord, please forgive us"

Crispin turned the lights back on and saw that Peter and Jimmy were still staring at the screen.

"Sorry about the beginning guys but I had to disguise the film a bit in case I got caught by the military." Crispin said.

"Crispin, what do you mean by getting caught by the military?" Peter asked.

"Guys, I'm on the run, I was given the task of processing the film and when I saw what the Manhattan Project was all about I knew I needed to do something about it and planned my get away. Officially I am visiting my brother in San Francisco who was Shot down last month over the pacific". Crispin explained.

"How, did you get away with that one, didn't they check to see if your story was true?" Jimmy asked.

"Luckily they didn't check on my story, I got in touch with a girl I know quite well who works at the military hospital, I got her to write me a letter to say that my brother was one of her patients and that he would possibly not recover from his injuries and if I wanted to see him I would have to come soon, I showed the letter to my boss and he ordered me to make my way to San Franciscan to see him."

Jimmy nodded as he listened to Crispin's plan but knew that he was lying.

"I just knew I had to get to you Jimmy, and that you would have the balls to do something about it." Crispin added.

"Ok, so we have made this bomb which will probably be a big problem for Japan come but what can we do about it now, the war is almost over apart from the imminent invasion of Japan, that's definitely going to be a bloody one, but it should be over soon, the Japanese military is almost completly destroyed anyway......

Crispin butted in. "Jimmy, there will be no invasion of Japan, the allies have decided that it will cause too many casualties and...."

Peter put his hand to his mouth... "They're not going to drop this thing on Japan to end the war are they?"

"I am afraid that exactly that is what is going to happen, a friend of mine who worked in the Post office at Los Alomos gave me a Telegram that was sent to one of the generals in charge explaining that he invasion was cancelled and that the new plan is to drop two atomic bombs on Japan to force the Japanese surrender."

"When will they be ready to use?" asked Peter.

"I have the Telegram here, the first attack will be on the 6 th of august and the second a few days later, weather permitting." Crispin added.

"Bloody hell, that's in a few weeks, so we wont have time to sabotage the attacks now and I suppose talking the government out of this would be like flogging a dead horse." Jimmy said.

"Most of the scientists are now against using these weapons, after realizing how devastating they are. There has already been a petition set up by Leo Szilard, one of the key Physicians to boycott the whole thing but it was turned down so it looks like many innocent people will perish or lose their homes."

"What do you mean by innocent people?" Jimmy asked.

"The bombs will be dropped on Hiroshima and Nagasaki, two towns that up until now are unscathed by the war and apart from a few small storage depots there are hardly any military in the area, we will be targeting innocent civilian people." Crispin said, his eyes now welling up with tears.

"If only we could get to Japan, fast, maybe we could inform them and get those towns evacuated before these terrible attacks happen." Crispin said.

Jimmy looked at Peter and began to smile, Peter smiled back.

"Guys, what the bloody hell have you got to smile about, hundreds of thousands of innocent people, women, children, the elderly, will be bombed using the most devastating weapon that has ever been developed, the only way we can do something about it is get to Japan as fast as possible...and you are smiling."

"Crispin, let's talk about the Project Peter and I have been working on."

Crispin was beginning to regret telling them of the Atomic bomb project and imminent attacks on Japan.

"Your project....who gives a monkeys about your bloody project... it think you guys haven't realized the problem here, and I think it was a mistake to let you in on this." Crispin said, his voice now becoming nervous.

"Every Problem has a solution and every solution problem, you can't have one without the other and believe me Crispin, your decision to come here and tell us about this problem was the best solution could have wished for.

Operation Silver Dove

Crispin stared at Jimmy with his mouth wide open, he then looked at Peter and back to Jimmy.

"So you have built a boat that can cross the Pacific in 8 days, it is only 20 meters long and carries a plane that it can catapult into flight, which can be picked up by a crane and bought back on deck?...that's bloody amazing!" Crispin said. Now smiling just as Peter and Jimmy had done a few moments earlier.

Jimmy Smiled back . "That's the best compliment I have received since Sally Braithwaite got a glimpse of my wedding tackle in the shower room of the rowing club back in the twenties." He said.

Peter looked at Jimmy and Smiled, and Jimmy winked back at Peter, who knew that a certain Sally Braithwaite had never existed and that Crispin was more Jimmy's type for an adventure between the sheets. Jimmy had confessed a year earlier to Peter that he was gay and all the nonsense abut getting in with the ladies was his way of covering up and dealing with it. Jimmy had been worried that his friendship with Peter would change after he had told him, which it did in a way. Their friendship became more solid and closer than before. They both knew now that they could trust each other no matter what and that was the icing on their friendship cake.

It meant a lot to Jimmy to be accepted by Peter and was happy to have found a true friend at last.

"So who is in charge of the project?" Crispin asked.

"Well actually that is me." Jimmy said looking very proud of himself.

Crispin smiled, "And how can we keep the fact that we want to use the Boat for an unofficial trip to Japan secret?" Crispin then asked with his eyebrows raised, with a "Lets see how you get out of this one Jimmy Blythe" look on his face.

Jimmy turned to Peter. "Peter, don't tell anyone we are going to steal our own Project, that nobody knows about anyway."

Peter nodded, and Jimmy turned to Crispin.

"Problem solved"

Crispin smiled at his colleagues.

"What do you mean by, nobody knows about it? In Los Alamos we have to fill in 4 forms in three different languages just to go for a pee and nobody talks about their work, nobody trusts anybody there."

"Well to be honest with you Crispin, nobody knows we are here, the Project we were working on was completed an autumn 1943 and we have been waiting to be disbanded and assigned to a new project ever since. About three months ago I rang up one the top knobs up at US government HQ and asked how I could get in touch with a certain Captain Jimmy Blyth in San Joakin Valley California and was told that I don't work here any more and have probably been sent back to Europe." Jimmy sat back in his seat smiling.

"So you have just been sat in this lovely little base, swanning around for a couple of years."

"Well not really swanning around, we built ourselves a perfect get away vessel." Peter butted in, pouring another coffee for all three of them.

The three began straight away to set up a plan.

Jimmy looked at his wristwatch that didn't exist.

"If CHD's info is right we have about twenty days before the attacks happen. We need eight days at full speed to get across the Pacific, lets say ten days just to be sure, if we leave the plane here we could probably save a day....." Jimmy looked at Peter who was shaking his head.

"I can cover the last two thousand Kilometres in the Kingfisher in a little less than seven hours at top speed, which means we reach the Japanese coast within six days of launching here, you guys will be nowhere near Japan and if we head for the north of the country there will be hardly any chance of meeting any military at all.

Most of the allied forces are in the south and Japan will be expecting an invasion from that direction."

Jimmy was staring at Peter and Crispin asked.

"Isn't there a chance you could get shot down? He asked.

"I will be flying very low, that makes me invisible to RADAR, most of the US Navy vessels are at least thirty meters high so that is what the Japanese in the area will be looking for, it would be terrible bad luck to be seen at all, let alone be shot at." Peter said. "The Kingfisher is fitted with the most modern surveillance equipment so I will see them long before they see me and if need be I can land on the water and move with the fitted outboard like a boat, almost totally silent and invisible."

Crispin nodded and was begining to like Peters plan but thought it a bit curios that Peter had seemed to have a plan to get to Japan already set up and ready to go.

Jimmy hadn't taken his eyes of Peter the whole time he was talking.

"But Peter.." Jimmy said his voice sounding dry and croaky, "If you fly 2000 Km at top speed in the Dove, the tank will be empty.... how will you be able to get back..."

Peter shrugged his shoulders.

"That is the risk I will have to take."

"Well let's not waste any time, Peter the Kingfisher
is fuelled up and ready for flight so I propose you
start up and fly over to Tomales Bay, Crispin and I
will use the Jeep." Jimmy said slurping the last of
his coffee down and standing up.

"What about rations and stuff like that?" Crispin
asked.

"There's enough Rations, Fuel and Water on board
to get us three times around the world and if need be
we could live on it for years without needing to stop
off anywhere for anything."

"You guys really have thought of absolutely
everything." Crispin Smiled, his smile truned into a
frown as he realized that what he had just said was
probably true. Peter and Jimmy didn't once seem to
be genuinley surprized about him turning up, and it
seemed to dawn on Crispin that they probably knew
about him coming all the time. He shook his head
and tried to get rid of the suspicious thoughts he was
having about his comrades as he and Jimmy watched
Peter take off and disappear into the distance before
jumping into the Jeep and making their way to
Tomales bay.

As Jimmy and Crispin approached the bay they saw
the Plane tied to a jetty, next to a small boat house.
Peter had already began getting the boat ready and
all they needed to do was haul the Kingfisher on
deck and start up the engines.

Peter was showing Crispin the Boat and how they winched the plane on deck while Jimmy looked out across the bay. Peter slowly drove the boat out of the Shed and Crispin fixed the Bow and Stern to the Jetty.

"All ready?" Jimmy asked.

"Eye Eye Cap'n." Peter replied.

Jimmy loosened the handbrake of the Jeep and let it roll down a steep bank next to the jetty, into the water.

He turned to Peter and Crispin.

"Let' get going guys, we have a job to do!" he bellowed with a huge smile on his face.

Crispin was amazed how fast the plane could be winched onto the deck and how easy the whole thing was to operate. And after a few minutes they were moving slowly through Tomales bay, heading for the open Pacific.

A few hours later the were well on their way and the coast of California was somewhere far behind the horizon. Jimmy was at the helm and Peter bought a fresh coffee into the control room.

"Once Peter is on his way, Crispin and I will head at very low speed toward the Philippines and when we are within rowing distance of the coast, we sink the boat, use the rescue dingy to row onshore and then make our way to Australia." Jimmy said.

"Why don't we just head for Guam? We would probably meet up with US Naval vessels and be picked up?" Crispin asked.

"CHD, my old friend, you are forgetting the fact that you are probably a wanted man, and a scientist that has been working on a project to build a horrendous bomb that will be dropped on Japan that goes missing and a few weeks later gets picked up by the military on his way back from the country that, that very military wanted to attack, CHD I don't think they will give you a heroes welcome. To be honest with you, I think the best thing is for you to disappear for a few years before showing your face again and Australia is a huge place and very good for hiding in. I have a friend up in the northern territories near Darwin, I will drop you off there before I make my way back to England and if anyone asks I will just say that the last time I saw you was back in Cambridge in the twenties when you left a rowing club party, three sheets to the wind after overfilling your bladder with G&T and that Peter and I were in the Pacific, testing the new system when he flew off and never came back, presumably shot down and missing at sea."

"I don't know anyone who can waffle his way out of a problem like you can." Peter said smiling at Jimmy, needing to change the subject.

"I am going to miss you my dear friend." Peter thought.

The weather was perfect for crossing the ocean and after five days they were approaching the spot where they would launch Peter in the Kingfisher. The three were sat on deck on the morning of the fifth day having breakfast, Jimmy looked out across the Pacific.

"We are a bit early, do you think we should wait another day before launching, the best time for the launch is eight in the evening, that way you reach the Japanese coast about four hundred kilometres north of Tokyo just before dawn?" Jimmy said.

"I leave this evening, we have no time to waste." Peter answered.

The rest of the day was spent setting up the Plane for launch, Crispin stowed the camera and film into a small watertight box in the main undercarriage float and for most of the afternoon they sat on deck, enjoyed their last day together and talked about the old days, the twenties in England, girls and rowing.

"I never thought that as an Oxford rower I would end up in a boat with two Rowers from Cambridge." Peter said smiling.

"Well don't tell anybody, it's probably against the law." Crispin answered.

"Yes I suppose it is, but if anyone asked us why we are together in this boat, I think they would understand our cause." Jimmy mentioned, playing with the beard that was slowly forming under his chin.

Crispin looked at his watch, "Four hours to the launch." He said, his voice now becoming quiet. Jimmy looked across at Peter for a second or two and when Peter looked in his direction there was a small moment where they looked each other in the eye but Jimmy quickly looked away.

"Well let's go though everything again, just to be sure that we haven't made any mistakes or left anything out of the plan." Jimmy said as he got up from the deck to make another coffee.

The four hours went by quicker than Peter expected and he was becoming more nervous the closer they got to the launch time. Jimmy had tried to avoid eye to eye contact with Peter all afternoon but now with only a few minutes to the launch of the kingfisher it was time to say their goodbyes.

Peter, dressed in his Oxford Rowing team Trousers and a thick tweed jacket made his way to the Kingfisher and stood on the main undercarriage float, pretending to check the plane over when Jimmy plucked up the courage and bellowed out.

"I refuse to let you get in that bloody plane without saying goodbye properly." His voice was breaking up and his eyes welled up with tears.

Peter waited a second or two and turned around to face Crispin and Jimmy, tears rolling down his face.

"I'm going to miss you my friend." He cried out.

Crispin nodded to Peter and a step back in respect and to give them a minute or two alone.

Jimmy held Peters shoulders and smiled, the tears now flowing at will.

"Are you scared?" He asked.

"I'm bloody petrified." Peter answered and they held on to each other and Crispin thought that they would never let go. "I wish you Godspeed my friend." Jimmy whispered and after a few seconds that felt like ten minutes Jimmy let go of his freind

"Right, let's get you off and on your way to Japan." He said.

Crispin came to Peter and shook his hand.

"You are the bravest man I have ever met and it is an honour to know you."

Peter nodded and patted Crispin on the shoulder then climbed into the cockpit of the Kingfisher, smiled and showed Jimmy the thumbs up.

There was a hissing sound and the Kingfisher was thrown forward, it dipped a few meters as it left the short catapult and Crispin raised his hands, thinking that Peter would crash onto the water but a second later he began to pick up speed and height.

Peter flew in a large circle and then past the boat fling a very low victory roll.

Jimmy and Crispin waved and Peter showed the thumbs up as he passed the boat and the two watched as the plane fly into the distance to become part of the horizon and dissapear, like the flowers and trees all those years ago on Peters journey in the Super Chief from Chicago to LA.

Once the Kingfisher was out of sight Jimmy turned to Crispin.

"Right, let's get on our way to Australia." He said.

Crispin looked Jimmy I the eyes, "Jim, I have a few open questions about this whole thing." He said quietly. "You guys didn't seem all that surpriesed when I turned up at San Joakin, to be honest it felt like you had been waiting for me to turn up with the film and when you just asked Peter if he was scared, and he replied that he was petrified, I didn't buy it Jim, what is going on here my friend?" Crispin asked.

Jimmy nodded and patted Crispin on the shoulder.

"Okay, it's time for the truth, lets set up the autopilot and I will tell you the whole story."

Jenny's last note

Denise arrived in LA and booked into a Hotel that was only a few hundred meters from the LA Times Building. She had absolutely no idea who she was going to get in touch with to find out more about her father , but thought that the Times was a good place to start. The following day she rang the reception and asked if there was anybody she could get in touch with. The reception lady informed her that the Times history office was the best bet and gave her the number.

The following morning she arrived at the times building early at eight o clock and she was led into in the small office where a young girl was waiting for her.

"Ah you must be Denise." the girl said.

"Yes that's me."

"Well come in and sit down, do you want a coffee, or tea?"

"Oh coffee would be lovely, with milk please."

"So your dad was Peter Marshall?" the girl asked, placing a huge mug of coffee on the desk next to Denise.

"Yes I think he worked from 1935 up until he left to work on a military project during the second world war and I am trying to find out what happened to him." Denise replied.

"Well, I know that he was very popular here at the times, always in a good mood and very kind and helpful, especially to the normal workers here at the times. I only have information for the time he spent here, after he left....well it was like he disappeared from the face of the planet. There was a rumour that he and Jenny Chandler had an affair but nobody could, or wanted to confirm that fact for me." The girl said.

"I can confirm that, Jenny was my mother, she gave me up for adoption and I grew up here in California before moving to England with my adoptive parents."

The girl shook her head and laughed out loud.

"Unbelievable, so it looks like I will have to change the history books."

She apologised to Denise for not being able to help and Denise explained that Peter had left LA to work on a military project and apparently went missing near the Japanese coast just before the end of the war and that she was hoping to fill in the missing link to try and find out what happened.

"I have a strange feeling that he wasn't shot down." Denise said.

The girl nodded, "I really am sorry I can't help you. She said.

Denise rang her friend Jane as soon as she was back in the Hotel room.

"I'm so disappointed Jane, I knew more about my father than they did." She explained, sounding very frustrated.

"Hey you haven't slept off you jet lag yet and you expect to find the holy grail within a few hours, spend some time in LA, go to places where he could or would have gone, talk to people about your dad, especially to elderly people, someone must have known him and maybe what happened, or where he was working on that project." Jane said.

"Yes you are right, I have to slow it down a bit and take my time, I will keep in touch Jane and if I need anything from England I will let you know.

After evening dinner Denise went back to her suite and fell fast asleep and didn't wake until the following day after breakfast. She sat up in bed and opened the bed side cabinet to stow some of her clothes away and saw a small black book.

"Why is there always a bible in hotel rooms in bedside cabinets?" she asked herself out loud, flipping through the pages, when small piece of crumpled paper fell out of the bible onto the floor, frowning she picked it up and read what had been written on it."

"The last weeks have been the best I have ever had, I will miss you my dear, San Joakin is not all that far away, I will visit you when I can."

Denise smiled, "Oh how sweet, a love letter." she said to herself, then she turned the crumpled paper around and her heart missed a beat when she read the words.

"To my darling Peter, my best friend and lover, yours forever, Jenny."

Denise wasn't sure if she would start laughing or crying and ended up doing both at the same time.

"Unbelievable, I am in the hotel that he lived in and in his suite, she put the note and bible onto the cabinet and went for a shower. Once dressed she made her way to the reception and then to the next cafe where she had a late breakfast and then made her way back to the suite as fast as she could to get in touch with the Military Historian office.

After explaining who she was she asked the man on the Phone if there was any information at all as to where he had worked during the war.

"Well it is very difficult to find that out, when the war ended, most of the documentation about scientist and their projects during the war was lost, often under suspicious circumstances. Possibly to protect the scientists but we don't know why really. Quite a lot of mysterious stuff went on back then and the fact that your Father was apparently lost at war we never got the chance to find out about what happened and where he was working." the Historian explained.

"I have been doing some research myself." Denise said. " I know he worked on some kind of plane, probably the reason they presume he was shot down and.... well it might sound strange but I believe I found a note in my hotel room, a love letter from his girl friend at the time which mentioned that he would be in San Joakin, I know it sounds like one of those love stories that come on the telly on Sunday evenings but its really true." Denise said.

"Believe me when I say, I have heard much more crazy things than that, let me have a look. Ah yes San Joakin Valley, there was a small airfield next to a large Military Depot where a Project to develop a surveillance air plane was carried out, it is possible that could have been your fathers project." the historian said. "Yes it was the Vought Kingfisher project, I am reading here about the base at San Joakin." The historian added. "A Plane that was fitted onto small speed boats and launched at sea using a catapult, yes it is quite possible that they were using that near the end of the war in the pacific theatre." He said.

The historian gave Denise the telephone number of the base and she hung up and rang the base.

She was informed that the base history room and museum was closed for two weeks as the lady that runs it is on vacation. Denise made an appointment directly on the Monday, two weeks later.

Fred

Denise looked out across Santa Cruz bay when a young girl came up to where she was sitting.

"Are we allowed to feed them?" the girl asked.

"I'm not sure dear, I am only looking after them for a few moments, the guy that works here will be back soon, we can ask him, I think he will probably allow you to help I'm sure." Denise answered and looked down at he three baby seals in the small shallow pool.

She had decided to take her time driving up to San Joakin valley and rented a mobile home to make her way up the Californian coast. She had a great time and now and then almost forgot why she was there in the first place, the last few hours was one of those instances.

She was approaching Santa Cruz that morning, when she saw a man on the side of the road with his head under the bonnet of his pick up truck, grey smoke was coming out from under the bonnet, engulfing him.

"Oh my god that cars on fire." she shouted to herself as She pulled over to help.

"Hello! Hello come a way from the car!" She yelled.

The man turned around, bumping his head on the bonnet of his car and smiled at Denise who was standing a few yards away with a fire extinguisher ready to attack the flames, he wiped his face with the back of his right hand which left an oil mark covering most of his left cheek, his long curly hair stuck to his sweaty face.

"Well if you can fix a burst radiator pipe with that extinguisher then feel free." he said with a strong Australian accent.

Denise frowned, then smiled and they spontaneously burst out laughing.

"You could help me though, my office is only a few kilometres from here, could you give me a lift? I'll get one of my mates to come down later and help me with my burning car." The man said smiling at the extinguisher.

"Oh by the way I'm Fred." he said as he opened the passenger door of her car.

" I'm Denise." She said.

Fred's office was very small and smelled of fish, it wasn't really an office but more a room where he could leave things lying around until they would be required or get thrown away.

"I would like to invite you for breakfast to say thank you for helping." Fred said as he rubbed the oil out of his face and had a strip wash using a bucket of water he had filled from one of the pools where baby seals were swimming around waiting for their breakfast.

Next to the sea life rescue station was a small Cafe and once he was cleaned up Fred bought them a few sandwiches and made a coffee. After breakfast Fred showed Denise around his workplace.

When he was finished showing her around he turned to her to thank her and say goodbye.

"Well I think I've bored you enough for now." He said

"No, not at all Fred, to be honest I am totally amazed what you achieve here all by yourself, but who looks after the animals when you are at home?" she asked.

Fred frowned. "Er, this is my home, there is a small room behind my office that I use as a bedroom that way I can be close to the animals. I am more or less their mother and father all in one, sometimes they cry out for me at night when the are hungry or scared. Three days a week I get help from the kids from a school just up the road here." He said opening the door of his bedroom.

"Er... there is nothing here." Denise said, looking baffled at Fred.

"I sleep on the Floor." He said.

"Fred, you need a good bed or you will end up with a bad back." she frowned at him.

"I have never slept in a bed in my whole life, I was found and bought up by an Aborigine Family in Australia." Fred replied

"My real mother had left me there knowing that they would care for me, she was probably too young or had some other problems and couldn't keep me." He added.

Denise told Fred about her story and that she was trying to find out what had happened to her father at the end of the war. They talked about his childhood and youth, his walkabout when he left the family that had cared for him and how he ended up in California.

"Do you still have contact with your family? " She asked.

"Oh yeah, we keep in touch and my Sister comes quite often, she lives and works in Dallas." Fred answered

One of Fred's friends turned up with a new Radiator pipe and they drove off to fix his car. Denise had offered to look after the animals together with three children from the school who had been there for the last few hours.

Denise stayed at the station all day, looked after the animals, helped Fred clean up and in the evening they sat together watching the sun set eating fried rice and vegetables that Fred had cooked for them. Once the sun had disappeared behind the horizon, Fred went into his bedroom and came out with what looked like a piece of tree trunk.

"I drum my babies to sleep each night." He said smiling and began to tap quietly on the drum. Almost instantly the Animals began to answer, with very quiet sounds, squeaking and howling noises came from the pools they were in. Fred constently slowed the rhythm of the drum beating and after a few minutes he tapped the drum about once every thirty seconds and eventually stopped, lay the instrument to one side and opened them both a beer. He saw the tears rolling down her cheeks and wiped his thumb across her face as he gave her a beer.

"That was the most beautiful thing I have ever experienced." Denise said and cuddled up to him.

They sat for a while without saying a word.

She wasn't sure how long they had been sitting there, without speaking when Fred slowly stood up and took her by the hand. They walked together toward his bedroom, both smiling at each other.

There was a swishing sound in on of the pools as a seal jumped around in the water and Fred stopped to listen.

"She is ready for freedom." He said and Denise Frowned.

"We will take her down to the beach tomorrow and let her go." He whispered as they walked into his bedroom and closed the door quietly behind them.

I come in Peace

Peter poured himself a black coffee out of the metal flask they had prepared before the launch and checked the cockpit dials of the Kingfisher.

"Hmm nothing to worry about." He said to himself quietly.

He checked his watch and the RADAR screen.

"Round about 150 Kilometres to go, a little over half an hour flying time ." He thought.

He thought about the mission and that the bombing of two cities that were of no strategical importance was probably made by some military generals and politicians who would be sleeping safe and sound in their beds when hundreds of innocent civilians, men women and children just trying to survive this terrible time, in a country that is already broken, would perish.

A short time later he checked the dials again.

"About 50 Kilometres to go." He said out loud and began to pull the Kingfishers controls to gain height. At 1000 Meters he levelled off and looked out toward the horizon.

The ocean was like a huge silver blanket, lit up by the moonlight. He still couldn't see the coastline although the RADAR showed that Japan was dead ahead. His heart missed a beat as the RADAR showed thee small green blips.

"Ships." he said quietly to himself and smiled.

 With only 20 Kilometres to the coast he saw more blips in the screen and could make out some vessels with the naked eye. Then he saw what looked like a huge black wave on the horizon.

"Japan." He said, smiling and lowered the Kingfisher back down to less than 10 Meters.

 He could now make out the coastline quite clearly, here and there the lights of small villages and houses were becoming more and more visible.

He turned the Kingfishers engine off and glided silently toward the Coast.

A few moments moment of complete and utter silence followed, before the plane gently glided onto the water that seemed to have been flattened out perfectly for him to land.

He glanced to the east, where the sky was beginning to change colour and it wouldn't be too long before the first signs of the new day would show themselves on the distant horizon.

A slight vibration of the controls and a whooshing sound of the main float on the water let him know that the plane had touched down. He waited for the plane to stop moving before turning on the small outboard motor that was fixed to the back of the main float and began silently to move toward the coast.

With a few hundred meters to the coast he opened the cockpit window and could hear the waves hitting the beach in front of him. He turned the outboard off ,climbed out of the cockpit and made his way down to the main float and opened a hatch where the small blow up dinghy was stowed. He pulled a chord and there was a short loud hissing sound as the dinghy filled with air. He fixed two oars to the dinghy which were also stored in the float and began to make his way to the beach.

As he approached the beach he could hear voices shouting and the sound of vehicles approaching.

He turned around and saw that there was only a few meters to go, he raised his hands to show that he wasn't armed and could now make out some Japanese soldiers that were pointing their guns in his direction.

"Watashi wa anshin shite kimasu" (*I come in peace*)Peter shouted.

He heard someone answer in Japanese but didn't understand a word as he got out of the dinghy and waded in the knee deep water the last few meters to the beach.

"Watashi wa anshin shite kimasu." he repeated. As he took the camera and film out of his Jacket pocket and kneeled on to the floor in front of the group of men.

"Watashi wa jujona joho o motte imnasu." (*I have important information for you*)

He stood back up, his hands raised above his head.

"Kono eiga o mitekudasai." *Please watch this film, it is important for the protection of civilians in the south of your country)*

One of the soldiers took a step toward him.

"I speak little English." He said and smiled at Peter who smiled back and nodded.

Peter bowed and the soldier bowed back.

"Please sir I have very important information that will protect civilians in the south of your country."

"Because of the invasion?" the soldier asked.

"No invasion is going to happen, I am afraid it is much worse than that, much worse than you can ever imagine." Peter said.

The soldier nodded and explained to his comrades what Peter had said, he picked up the camera and film and held a hand out to Peter.

"Come with us." the soldier said.

<u>Sakura</u>

Peter was taken by the soldiers to a small army camp not far from the beach where he had come ashore and by the look on the faces of some of the soldiers he was sure he would either be executed, or even worse he could end up in Unit 731 where anything imaginable could happen to him. He tried not to think of the worst case scenarios.

The main Problem that Peter had, was that only one soldier here in this Camp knew the whole story as to why he was here, the one that could speak good Enblish that picked up the camera on the beach. But it would only take one soldier with a loaded gun, a moment of hate or madness and he was a dead man for sure, but he also knew it would only be a matter of time and he would be safe.

He was taken to a building and into a large room with tables and chairs and a large white wall at one end.

The English speaking soldier explained that he could use the wall as a screen to show the film and that the camp commandant would arrive shortly.

A few minutes later two officers arrived and somebody shouted out an order, the soldiers stood to attention before one of the officers nodded and told everybody to relax. He then gestured Peter to show the film.

Peter nodded in agreement and set up the camera on a table next to where the officers were sat when a soldier who had been guarding the door came and mumbled something to one of the officers.

Peter only understood the words "Sakura Funayama" at the end of the sentence.

The soldier gave an order and a woman entered the room, bowed to the officers and sat down next to Peter.

I am Sakura, I can speak English and they have rudely awoken me to translate." She said, looking very cross at Peter.

Peter nodded and smiled. She had long wavy black hair and soft facial contours and smelled of lavender, he realised that she had been watching him the whole time and he was instantly embarrassed, clumsily knocking over the camera. Sakura smiled and he smiled back.

"Please tell them that the beginning is a Walt Disney film, we had to disguise it in case we were captured by allied forces."

Sakura leant over, putting a hand on Peters thigh and explained to the officers what he had said.

As the film started, some of the soldiers began to smile and snigger and Sakura held a hand in front of her mouth and looked at Peter with one eyebrow raised.

Then the film, and the faces of everyone on the room changed as the words

"Manhatten Project – Trinity test" came up on the screen.

They saw soldiers standing around a large bomb that was in a kind of scaffolding and shortly after saw a huge explosion.

The film lasted fifteen minutes and showed the detonation from different angles, and how houses, vehicles and animals were either destroyed by the huge blast or incinerated instantly by the heat caused by the bomb.

The film ended and one of the soldiers turned the lights back on.

Peters eyes were welling up with tears as he turned to the officers, who were , like most people who watch the Trinity test for the first time, in total and utter shock at what they had just witnessed.

Peter touched the arm of the officer sat next to him who was still staring at the wall although the film had ended.

"Please evacuate Hiroshima and Nagasaki, we have information that Hiroshima will be bombed on the 6th of august and Nagasaki shortly after that, the allies want to demonstrate that they can destroy your country."

Once Sakura had explained to the officer what Peter had said he ordered a soldier to take the film and camera, he than turned to Sakura and spoke to her for a few minutes , she nodded and turned to Peter.

"They will now inform the top local general about the film and your message, you will be held here in the camp as a guest and he has appointed me to look after you."

Peter nodded to the officer who then stood up and saluted Peter who also stood up and bowed.

"I will take you to the mess building where you will be staying." Sakura said and gestured Peter to follow her.

The mess building was next to the cookhouse of the small camp where he had shown them the film. The room was more like a prison cell than a mess bedroom. A sleeping mat on the floor with some blankets, a small table with a chair.

"The shower room is just down the corridor on the left, I will bring you some fresh clothing, you are about the same size as my brother." Sakura said, and Peter nodded in agreement.

"I will bring you some rice porridge and tea, then at ten o clock we have an appointment at the camp commanders office, on of the top generals who is based not far from here is already in his way."

Sakura looked nervously toward the door and then turned to Peter and kissed him on the cheek.

Peter took a step backward, an astonished look on his face and Sakura smiled nervously. Peter frowned and took a step toward Sakura, she held a hand to his mouth as they heard footsteps in the corridor.

"I wanted to show my thankfulness, my sister lives in Nagasaki with her Family, I will inform them to come here until this is all over." She said.

Peter nodded "Good." he said.

Peter slept for a few hours and was awoken by a quiet knocking on the door to his room and Sakura walked in. Her hair was now pinned up in the traditional Japanese way and she emptied a bag of clothes onto the small table in his room.

A white shirt, black trousers and a black jacket, a towel, soap and some mint paste so he could have a shower.

After showering and getting dressed in the clothes she had brought he went back to his room where Sakura had laid out the table for breakfast and stood up as he came into the room.

"Looks delicious" he said as Sakura surprised him with another kiss.

"And who was that one for?" he said.

"That one was for me." she said sniggering cutely, "I was in a bad mood when the woke me but I am feeling better now." She said as she turned to open the window.

Peter held her arm and she turned back to face him, he kissed her gently on the lips and Sakura looked nervously again at the door.

"Who was that one for." she whispered, smiling.

"That one was for us." He said.

The commandant was sat behind a huge desk that reminded him of the one in Jenny chandlers office in LA. Two other officers, one of them the local General, were sat with their backs to the door of the office, as Sakura and Peter entered the room all three stood up to salute Peter, who bowed to the men.

"I am not a military man but I expect the saluting is a form of showing respect." Peter said

Sakura translated to the officers who smiled and nodded and the general said a few words to Sakura.

"He said that he will be glad when this bloody war is over so he can burn this stinking uniform." she said to Peter.

Peter nodded and held out a hand to the General who shook Peters hand, it seemed to the others in the room that they were not meeting for the first time and the Camp commandant watched the two closeley and as they sat down there was a short moment when Peter and the General looked each other in the eye as if they were old friends seeing each other again for the first time in years.

The Commandant watched them nod and smile at each other. He shook his head at the thought and sat down.

"Our intelligence have confirmed that your story is true, the allies have the bomb and at least two of them have been transported to Tinian island just north of Guam and it looks like they will be ready for use soon. We have begun to plan the evacuation of Hiroshima and Nagasaki and will try to get as many civilians away from those cities as we possibly can. One thing we didn't know was how devastating these weapons are. Peter your film gave us very important information and we are very thankful." The General said in almost perfect English nodding to Peter and then translated what he had said into Japanese for the others in the room.

Sakura, the camp commandant and other officer didn't seem to realize that the General had called Peter by his first name and Peter tried not to show any surprize.

"You can stay here in Japan as a guest of our country as long as you wish and I propose that Sakura should look after you to make sure you don't get up to mischief." the Genral explained.

"If you require any further help just let me know." Peter said.

Sakura and Peter went back to his room and gathered the rest of his belongings before leaving the camp and making their way to the small village where she lived.

Roger Blythe

Denise arrived back home in Manchester on a typical grey rainy day and was missing California and Fred already. As soon as she arrived home she got in touch with Brian in London and told him to send one million pounds to a Sea animal rescue station in Santa Cruz in California as an anonymous donation.

She had told Fred about why she was in America and had said that it was important for her to find out what had happened to her father before she moved to America to live with him but he hadn't told him of her wealth and had decided to keep it secret until she was back together with him.

The appointment in the base at San Joakin Valley had been very successful and the old lady who ran the History room had known Jimmy Blythe and Peter very well as she had worked in the officers mess there during the war. She explained about the day Crispin turned up and how the three of them made their way to the Hangar where the Kingfisher was kept, that the curtains closed and shortly after she had heard the Kingfisher taking off and never saw the three of them again after that day...... until a summers day in 1985 when Jimmy Blythe and his nephew Roger turned up at the History room totally out of the blue.

Jimmy had explained about the mission they had gone on after finding out about the Atomic bomb attacks. That he and Crispin had made their way to Australia where they both lived on a farm near Darwin in the Northern territories. Jimmy moved back to the UK in the seventies when Crispin his friend and partner died. Jimmy had also said that Peter was alive and had lived in Japan the whole time but unfortunately she had no further information and said to Denise that she should try and get in touch with Roger Blythe, Jimmy's nephew as he would definitely know the full story. He said he was in the Army.

"I think he said the Welsh Guards was his regiment." Was the last thing the lady said as she walked Denise back to her car

Denise thanked the lady for the information, and after spending a few days with Fred, made her way back to England.

Roger Blythe who was now a retired Brigadier and lived near Nottingham was delighted when Denise got in touch.

"Oh that's a nice surprise" He said as he answered the phone.

"Yes, Jenny Chandler died a while ago and I had no idea that I was adopted until I received the will." Denise explained and began to ask Roger about Jimmy and her Father.

"Lets not do this on the phone, I would like to invite you down here to my place for a day, that way we can take our time and read Jimmy memoirs together." Roger said.

"Oh he wrote his memoirs?" she asked.

"Yes, very interesting too, explained the whole thing and there is a lot about your Dads time before they met up again at San Joakin Valley, and of Crispin and his time at the Manhattan Project."

"Denise Lawrence, the daughter Peter Marshall didn't get to see... up until now anyway.? Roger Blythe smiled at Denise sitting in one of the chairs in his conservatory as he poured them a cup of tea, two weeks after Denise had got in touch with him.

 "Up until now?" Denise butted in..."do you mean he is still alive?" She frowned.

"Oh yes he's alive and well dear, I talked to him on the phone yesterday and told him you will be coming down here to see me."

Denise had a look of shock on her face.

"Er..where is he, how can I get to him....I..."Denise stuttered.

"First things first dear, lets go through the whole story before you make your decision ." Roger said holding a hand up to slow and calm Denise down. Denise frowned again and shook her head as if to ask why and Roger nodded and opened a large brown envelope.

Before he began reading he looked at Denise, your father was the one that made the decision for you to be adopted, Jenny had visited him at San Joakin when she was about seven months pregnant with you....he didn't change his will, although he could have done so, Jenny wanted to keep you but respected his descision and give you up for adoption.

She married shortly after the war and wrote the Will to pass on Peters assets to you.

 Do you still want me to carry on?" Roger said.

"Yes please read on." She said, a tear rolling down her face as she now realized that she had been wrong all the time and that Jenny had only given her up for adoption because Peter had insisted on it.

"He said to me that it was important for you to know that, so that you can make the decision to see him or not, knowing the full truth." Roger added.

Three hours later Roger put the memoirs back into the envelope and turned to Denise who was just staring into nothing, shaking her head slightly.

"So Jimmy and Peter had planned to get away from America the whole time and secretly built a getaway ship and Plane while in San Joakin Valley?" Denise stared now at Roger.

"And that Crispin making his way to San Joakin after seeing the Film of the Trinity Test was a set up?"

"Yep, while your dad was working for the LA Times he was friends with many scientists who were working on products that he wrote about. One of those scientists was Leo Szilard, one of the key scientists who would later work on the Manhattan Project during the war. After telling Jimmy and Peter about the bomb they were making they persuaded Leo to try and boycott the whole thing by setting op a petition, a petition would have probably never have worked but the background idea was that scientists working on the project would realize how dangerous the bomb was and boycott the whole thing internally. In the Spring of 1945 there were still a lot of unanswered questions in the development of the atomic bomb and it would have been quite easy for the scientists working on certain unanswered questions to take their time, or just not find answers. Unfortunately it was fear that caused them not to boycott the Project in the end. It wasn't unusual for Scientists to just disappear or die after a tragic accident when the powers that be found out that they were against the project. When the Petition was shown to the top military Generals in Los Alamos it was thrown straight into the bin, however most of the scientists had found out about the petition and there was a real fear of a revolution within the Los Alamos Project. More scientist began to disappear or have tragic accidents in the Lab or car crashes. Military control of the Project was becoming more intense as time went on and the scientists were watched very closely and it was the simple fear of losing their lives that kept them working on the atomic bomb."

Denise shook her head, "But how did Crispin know that he had to get in touch with Jimmy and Peter, the only two people on the planet at the time that could do anything about the Bomb?"

"Well that was quite easy really, Crispin was given the task of producing Films and documenting progress on the Testing of the weapons, it was touch and go really, they knew that once the bomb was tested that it would only be a matter of weeks before it would be dropped on Japan, the allies had been planning a dummy Invasion on Japan the whole time to keep the general interest away from what was going on way behind their own lines, back home. Crispin worked together with two Scientists in a small building near a guardroom, now and then they would be visited by a soldier who was interested in photography and filming. Crispin and his colleagues thought that the soldier was just keeping an eye on them. Which he was in a way,the soldier was cousin of Peter, his job was to get a copy of the film of the first test of the bomb and to persuade Crispin to get the information to Jimmy and Peter who were just waiting for him to turn up really."

Denise laughed and shook her head, "Are you trying to tell me that my Father was a spy?"

"I don't need to try hard Denise, because that is what he was. Crispin was persuaded by Peters cousin to take the film to somebody who he could trust and would want to do something about it knowing full well that Jimmy would be Crispin's choice, he pretended to find out Jimmy's whereabouts, something he knew all along, and helped him get out of Los Alamos and to San Joakin Valley. With the Film and the information they could then make their way to Japan where Peter would fly the last 2000 Kilometres alone in the Kingfisher and never be seen again."

"But howe could he know where to go to in Japan, he could have quite easily have been shot down or....." Denise stopped talking when she realized that Roger was smiling with ine eyebrow raised.

"He landed as planned about four hundred kilometres north of Tokyo, the chance of getting shot down was more or less non existent, to be sure though the Japanese sealed off that part of the coast with military coastguard ships and in the welcome committee on the beach, was a Japanese soldier who could speak a few words of English, actually he was bloody good at speaking English, he studied together with Peter in Oxford and his job was to make sure Peter got to the camp safe and sound so he could show the film of the Trinity test, he was also responsible for getting the information to the local General who would then inform the Powers that be to evacuate the drop zones of the bombs.

The General, who was a schoolfriend of Peter called Kishiro and grew up with him in Chicago was their key person in Japan."

Denise stared out of the conservatory into Rogers garden. and shook her head.

"Kishiro's father was a cook and his mother worked nights in a laundry, they were poor and were having problems making ends meet while Peters father was one of the top Architects in California, Peter looked after his friends family, bought them food when they had nothing to eat and even money to help them out. When the second world war broke out Kishiro went back to Japan and promised his father that he would look after the rest of the family there, who lived in the far north of the country. Peter and Kishiro had made up a language of their own whilst growing up so they could communicate without others knowing what they were on a bout, something they did for fun as kids, saved hundreds of thousands of Japanese civilians in the last days of the war."

"They kept in touch the whole time using their made up Language and Morse code, they organised Peter's arrival in Japan and the evacuation of Hiroshima and Nagasaki. Of course Peter had to stay in Japan after the war. There was no way he would or could have gone back to America, even if he had wanted to. Kashiro was the Mayor of a town not far from where Peter landed and was given the Military rank of General during the war, he made sure that Peter could stay on Japan, they changed his Name to Pita and he married Sakura, the translator who he met the night he landed in Japan."

Denise smiled at Roger with raised eyebrows..

"No.. no.... that was probably the only thing that wasn't planned, it was love at first sight...true and real."

Roger rubbed his eyes....

"It's time for my afternoon nap." He said.

"Yes I have to make my way back to Manchester, I will try and get the three o Clock train." She said as Roger took her to the front door of his house and gave her a small envelope.

"I think you have already made up your mind... but here's all the information you need to get in touch with Peter and Sakura anyway." He said smiling.

Denise kissed Roger on the cheek.

"Thank you." she whispered and made her way to the bus stop.

"So it was Peter who didn't want me and not Jenny." She thought as she waited for the bus.

She looked at the unopened envelope and another tear rolled down her cheek.

Roger was right, she had already made her decision.

Tears for a Hero

It was a warm spring day in 2005 and although not yet in bloom, the cherry trees in and around the cemetery were beginning to show signs of appreciation and thankfulness for the first warm weeks of the year. Here and there, the dark brown cherry blossom buds were beginning to show colour and Ichika turned to her mother Sakura.

"Look mum the dahlias are blooming now where his cross used to be".

"Yes it must have been about here, just next to the third cherry tree after the wooden bench." Her mother replied.

"How many years have we been coming here?" asked Ichika.

"Oh, he died in 1998 so this will be the seventh time including the day we lay him to rest." Sakura answered, a tear now rolling down her cheek as she brushed a hand through the flowers where his wooden cross used to be.

It was tradition that a small wooden cross was placed and flowers were planted where people from the village were laid to rest and after a few years, when the cross was long gone, the flowers would mark the place where the graves were.

"My Peter, love knows no boarders or conditions and no pain can be worse than the pain in my heart now that you are not here with me." Sakura said and brushed though the flowers again as if she was ruffling his hair as she used to to every morning when they awoke.

"One day soon, we will unite." She said smiling, as she turned to her daughter. Her smile turned to a questioning frown.

"Where's my daughter Ichika?" She asked.

"Oh she went back to the car, she had an important call to answer." Answered Ichika.

She had begun to understand her mothers Alzheimer and had stopped trying to explain who she was every five minutes and pretended to be someone else that Ichika had sent to look after her. It was less confusing for her mum and usually after a few minutes things would be back to normal anyway. Sometimes Ichika wondered how her mother could remember her husband Peter at all, and recite the funeral speech she wrote for him seven years ago, every year when they visited his grave on his birthday and the wonderful story of how her mother and father had met all those years ago, her mother knew everything like it had happened yesterday.

Ichikas half sister, Denise had walked a little further up the hill to take Photographs of the Cherry trees, turned and saw Ichika and Sakura making their way

Toward the main gate of the cemetery, Ichika beckoned her to follow and Denise hurried back down the hill and caught up with the others as they reached the car. A few moments later they were driving though the village where Ichika and her Mother now lived.

"It was here in this village on the beach where we met for the first time, all those years ago." Sakura said looking out of the window pointing at the houses rushing by, it is a wonder that we fell in love at all, I had just been woken up and my hair was all a mess and he stunk of sweat, fish and seawater." She added, Denise and Ichika burst out into spontaneous laughter.

Denise then touched Ichika's arm to get her attention.

"Here in this Village, wasn't it four hundred kilometres north of Tokyo on the other side of the country?" she askled.

"Ichika nodded and poked with a finger at the side of her head, "Alzheimer." She said and Denise nodded.

"I didn't fall in love with his body, although he was a damned good looking son of a gun." Sakura carried on speaking from the back seat of the car. Ichika and Denise looked at each other and started sniggering again.

"It was his courage, he risked his own life to save all those people who didn't want anything to do with all that dreadful fighting, people like your father, they are the real heroes girls, never forget that." She said as Ichika pulled into a parking place at the restaurant they traditionally ate each year after visiting Peters grave.

Denise helped Sakura out of the back seat of the car who turned to look out across the ocean and took a deep breathof fresh sea air.

"This is where the mess hall used to be." she said, pointing to a small grassy area next to the car park.

"Yes it looks nice now, with the grass and flowers.

"All gone to flowers, so peaceful and quiet, just like his grave, let's hope it stays that way." Sakura said,

As they reached the door of the restaurant she turned to Denise.

"Everything goes to flowers eventualy when left in peace." She said.

Pita Funayama

Yakushima Island 1965

The group of children shouted at Pita again as loud as the could.

"Hey he's coming back" they cried and Pita could hear his daughters voice much louder than the others as he turned to face the man that was preparing to attack him once again.

The man wielded a black metal pole in one hand and the other hand was balled in a fist, and was ready for the fight to continue. He began to wave the black pole furiously as he moved forward. Pita took a step back and moved his right arm in a large circular motion to block the attack, he then swung his left arm in the same way and in an instant had his attacker in a painful restraining hold. The attacker cried out in pain and dropped the pole, Pita applied a little more pressure in the hold and the man held up his free hand in surrender.

"Okay, okay I give up...I surrender."

Pita let go of the man and they turned to the audience, the children all sitting cross legged on the floor, their parents stood behind them.

The Aikido demonstration was always the big attraction at the school open day. Pita was the head of Sport and discipline and also taught Physics and English, his wife Sakura taught Literature and History at the school.

"Okay children, now I had the attacker in a restraining hold, what do I do next, anyone got an idea?"

"I know what to do daddy." his daughter Ishika shouted, a hand raised as high as she could.

Pita nodded and beckoned his daughter so stand up and then raised his eyebrows signalling his Daughter to speak.

Ishika stood up and brushed her wavy long black hair out of her face, Pita was exploding with pride.

"I would punch him on the nose!" She shouted.

The whole audience burst out into spontaneous laughter and Sakura covered her mouth to hide her smile.

Pita smiled too and shook his head.

"Well yes you could of course punch him on the nose, he definitely would have deserved it but that would be Karate and not Aikiodo.

"Children, we practice and use Aikido to neutralize our attacker and make it impossible for them to carry out any further aggressive attacks, without injuring them.

With Aikido we demonstrate how powerful we are without seriously hurting our opponent, and once we have neutralized the attack, we use our most powerful weapon that we have."

Pita raised his eyes again, this time to the whole group as if to ask which weapon he was talking about.

"Communication!" the children sang out together.

"Yes, well done." Pita replied. "We communicate, calm our aggressor down and talk them into a peaceful agreement."

One of the parents then shouted out.

"And what if that doesn't work?"

"Well then you can punch him on the nose and run away." Pita replied and the room burst into laughter and applause.

Later that evening Sakura and Pita sat in the front garden of their house after putting Ishika to bed.

"She is so much like you it is unbelievable." Sakura said.

"Her character, yes, but she looks more like you every day, I love the way she brushes her fringe out of her face, just like you do." Pita replied.

There was a pregnant pause in the conversation then Sakura asked.

"Have you heard anything new about Denise?" Sakura sked.

"Jimmy rang the other day, he keeps in touch with Bill and Katy Lawrence for me, they have now moved to Manchester in England, she is almost 22 years old now." He said.

"Maybe one day you will see her again." Sakura said.

"Yes that will happen when the right time comes, I am sure." Peter replied.

Sakura kissed Peter lovingly on the cheek, "Lets have a walk through the village before it gets dark." She said.

After a few hundred meters they sat on a wooden bench and looked out into the bay and ocean beyond.

"I hope it stays this peaceful." Sakura whispered.

Peter looked across the Pacific that was slowly turning colour, he looked up at the full moon, the ocean would soon the same silver grey as it was all those years ago when he arrived in the Kingfisher. He took a deep breath.

"I hope so too." he said.

Operation Rolling Thunder

The following morning in Vietnam, was the day Operation rolling thunder began. 100 U.S fighter bomber aircraft attacked targets in the north of the country. Although planned only to last 2 months, the operation went on for three years and over three million sorties were flown, dropping almost 8 Million tons of bombs **four times the tonnage of bombs that were dropped during the whole of the second world war, worldwide.**

The majority of the bombs were dropped on south Vietnam, targeting the Vietcong and North Vietnamese military who had advanced into the south, which caused almost 3 Million casualties and refugees.

The north Vietnamese Military and Vietcong reacted by decentralizing their main Positions and depots away from civilian built up areas and farmland where it was possible.

A decision that was made to protect the civilian population, lowering the civilian casualty and refugee count to almost none for the rest of the Vietnam war.

The Deadliest war in History

It is estimated that more than 100 Million people perished during world war two from 1939 to 1945.

In the strategic bombing raids carried out on many cities worldwide during the war, it was the civilian working class and their homes that were deliberately targeted and it is estimated that more than twice as many civilians died during the war than military personnel. There were also millions of deaths caused by malnutrition and disease as a direct knock on effect of the bombing of cities.

There were many attempts to find a peaceful solution and to protect civilian lives.

Rudolph Hess, Hitler's right hand man in the Nazi party who flew alone to Great Britain in 1941, trying to find a peaceful solution to the conflict in Europe.

The story of Oskar Schindler was made famous by the filming of Schindlers List and thousands of families Europe wide, tried to protect their Jewish friends and Neighbors from the Nazi party. Many were successful but trajicaly more than half of the Jews being protected by friends and neighbours were caught and either executed on the spot or sent to concentration camps to die. The Anne Frank story tells the tale of one of those attempts that unfortunately failed.

Many political attempts were also made to try and change the course of the war and find a peaceful end.

One of these failed attempts was the Szilard Petition when 70 scientists involved in the development of the Atomic Bomb, realizing how devastating these weapons would be, attempted to boycott the project.

The Title of the book "Gone to Flowers...everyone" and the poem "The peace child" were inspired by the last verse of the folk song.

Where have all the flowers gone .

The current global situation

In 2020, almost 75 Years after the end of World War Two, there are over 200 Countries officially at war.

*Those defined as "**at war**" are countries whose ongoing conflicts have caused **at least 1000 deaths** in the current or past year. Fatality figures include only those who die in combat **and civilians intentionally targeted**, the deaths, injuries and refugees caused by the knock on effect of these conflicts are never documented but it is estimated that several million civilians die, become injured or lose their homes each year due to ongoing conflicts.*

The question, "when will we ever learn?" will more than likely never be answered.

About the author

Stephen Moralee was born in an Army camp in the south of England and spent his childhood in Germany where his father was based as an Army soldier. Stephen also joined the Army at the age of 16 and experienced active service twice in Northern Ireland and in Operation Desert Storm in 1991

After experiencing war at first hand, he began to wonder if being a soldier was the right profession for him and he eventually ended his army career in 1993.

in 2017 he became ill with the auto immune disease Transverse myelitis which left him mostly paralysed in 2018 he took up writing as a new hobby and published his first book in 2019. Later that same year he was diagnosed with with a second autoimmune disease Multiple Sclerosis, Chronic Fateagie Syndrom and Post Traumatic Stress disorder.

He lives in Kamen in Germany with his family where he works as a freelance artist and music producer.